NIGHT OF THE FLAMING GUNS

NIGHT OF THE FLAMING GUNS

P. A. Bechko

CHIVERS LARGE PRINT
BATH

British Library Cataloguing in Publication Data available

This Large Print edition published by Chivers Press, Bath, 1994.

Published by arrangement with the author.

U.K. Hardcover ISBN 0 7451 2281 7

All of the characters in this book are fictitious,
and any resemblance to actual persons,
living or dead, is purely coincidental.

Photoset, printed and bound in Great Britain by
Redwood Books, Trowbridge, Wiltshire

NIGHT OF THE FLAMING GUNS

CHAPTER ONE

When I finally reached Tucson I felt like I was hauling half the dust of the desert along with me. My face was feeling pinched and gritty. My eyes were red-rimmed and felt like they'd dried up on me. It was 1878, getting on into summer, and three days on the trail did a lot to take the starch out of most any man, even one who'd spent as much time in wild country as I. The desert was like an oven and dust devils sprung up from the desert floor to dog a man's heels almost like they was alive and took pleasure in worrying a body. That burning sun bleached out everything, a man's clothes, his gear, his hair, and even his brains it seemed like. I was just up from Fort Buchanan to the south, and glad to be shut of it. I'd been doing some scouting for the Army. Things went smooth enough at first, but when that major started to ordering me around like one of his soldier boys in that low, gravelly voice of his, I drew what pay I had coming and lit out for other parts. It was just as well. That major and me, we got along like two tomcats tied up together in a canvas bag. 'Sides, the way those Apache were raiding and those soldier boys were playing at soldiering, I didn't see how that fort could stick out there anyhow,

1

and I didn't want my hair hanging from some lodgepole to dry. I'd been up around Fort Reno, Wyoming, a couple years back, in '76, when word come down about Custer and the Sioux at the Little Big Horn. Seemed to me that these were considerably different circumstances, but the men at Fort Buchanan were heading for the same disaster. Now I was a big man, not overly tall, but big enough so's it was hard to go unnoticed by them Indians out there. Scouting was my living at the time, not soldiering, and I didn't figure on getting myself killed for some major with rocks for brains ...

I climbed down off'a my roan in front of the saloon, my clothes stiff with a mixture of sweat and sand, my bones weary of the saddle, and looped the reins over the hitching post. The Fourth of July was coming up in a couple days if I recalled rightly, and by the sound of things the boys in the saloon were already working themselves up to it. Some glass crashed loudly inside, followed by the sound of splintering wood and the hoarse cheers of the local onlookers. I'd been in and witnessed enough barroom brawls to know the sound of one when I heard it. I would'a just as soon stepped around it, this time leastways, but I had me a powerful thirst. I needed something to cut the desert dust in my throat, and that couldn't wait. Looking over the top of the batwings a couple of seconds got me a fast look at the pair that were having at it inside. Through the heavy, smoky haze I could see it wasn't an even match. One was square and stocky, and the other tall and slim. Reckon the taller one was giving away thirty or forty pounds to the stockier one. The thinner one, he all of a sudden found himself picked up by the collar and the seat of the pants, heading for the door. I opened the half of the batwings I'd been leaning on. The taller fighter went right on past me, off the boardwalk and into the dusty street. He laid there a second, kind of dazed like, shaking his head like a wounded bull, then climbed unsteadily to his feet, and staggering a mite headed back inside. I opened the door for him the second time, and followed him on inside. Slipping off to one side, I worked my way past the shouting, swaying crowd and through the thick screen of smoke, around to the bar as the fight got started again. It was a friendly fight, but I didn't want no part of it right now, and it was all fired easy to get dragged into them things when folks got to roughhousing.

Something crashed on the far side of the room, but I couldn't see what it was because the rest of the men in the bar had closed in a tight circle around the contestants. Getting the barkeep's attention took some little doing. He was more interested in the fight than some business, but when he finally noticed me, he come down my way with a broad grin spread across his thin face. He was kind of tall and wiry looking with a hard, lined face and a black mustache. I recognized him right away; he went by the name of Turk Billings. Last time I saw him he had himself a little bar down on the waterfront back in New Orleans. Turk was a mad grizzly of a man in a fight and it didn't take much to get him going. Thing of it was, he had him a soft spot for strays, and it wasn't so long ago that I was one of 'em. It was him that was there when I needed a friend some years back at a time when I had more trouble than one kid had a right to have. This here was a man I owed, though neither of us ever talked about it.

I'd heard tell he'd got himself a hankering for the wideopen spaces, but it beat all how a man could wander up one side of the country, and down the other and still manage to run into folks he knew. I shook his hand and grinned right back at him.

'Turk, you ol' son.' Seeing Turk made me feel some better, putting that hard trail behind me.

It should have been considerable cooler in the saloon than outside, being as it was made of adobe. Trouble was, even that adobe wasn't no match for a bunch of sweaty, cigarette puffing cowhands. Fact was, it was hot in there, and the blanket of smoke stifling. The light of the desert sun streamed through the windows, knifing through the dim room.

'Matt Logan! Heard you were scouting out of Fort Buchanan,' he said, releasing his grip on my hand and drawing me a beer. Them cool, gray eyes of his looked me up and down real good. 'It appears you've had a long, dusty ride, my friend.'

Me, I knew what I looked like. The others in the saloon were in town for a couple of days of fun. I was fresh off the trail, and wasn't very handsome to begin with.

There was a cracking, crashing sound from the far corner as a chair gave way beneath the combined weight of the fighters. When I looked up, I could see the pair still fighting, but what caught my eye was a pair of crossed swords hanging on the wall. Turk'd had the same ones back in New Orleans. Talk there was his daddy had been a pirate. Knowing Turk, that wasn't too hard to believe.

'Don't that bother you none?' I used my beer glass to point in the general direction of the fight.

Turk grinned. 'Hell no. There's this character named Flannigan. He's Irish or something. Runs the Flying L spread about two days' ride west of here. These are his

5

boys, and he stands good for the damages. Says living out in the middle of nowhere the way they do, fighting Apache to keep that spread going, they need a little relaxation. That's the way he puts it, and as long as he comes up with the hard cash to cover the damages, I've got no argument with him.' Turk ran a hand through his black hair, like he was scratching his head. It didn't do him no good though, I'd already seen the bald spot he was trying to hide.

Me, I just leaned back against the bar, took a long pull on my beer and grinned, for this was that kind of country. Tucson was a raw, wild frontier town, and while it had its share of good folks, mostly it had a bunch of curly wolves hunting for a place to howl. You couldn't blame folks for living thataway. It was a wild time, and most figured you'd better live for today, a body couldn't really count on being around to see tomorrow.

Glancing up into the large mirror behind the bar, I saw my own eyes staring back at me. I needed a bath and a shave. I caught sight of that fight heading back our way. I hopped up on the bar dropping down on Turk's side as the pair lunged past, falling to the floorboards and rolling together like a pair of bear cubs in play.

'Didn't want to spill my beer,' I said lightly. 'Seems like old times, there never was a dull minute at that waterfront bar back

6

in New Orleans neither as I recall.' Turk was a man who went in for the rough stuff. First time I met him had been years ago when he'd been running a bar, catering to the river men. Men who worked the great Mississippi. The men on the river had been Turk's kind just as these men were … men who were strong enough to settle the West.

Turk shrugged. 'Man's got to keep his hand in.'

The fight sort of wore itself out in the far corner and the men started drifting back to the bar and tables to finish their drinks and order more. My eyes sort of wandered around the place while Turk tended bar. I spotted a few familiar faces. Not those of men I knew personally, but men with reputations. A celebration usually drew everything the country had to offer, and this one would be no exception. There was one man who sat alone. He was Mexican and he was called Diego. I'd never heard a last name. I'd heard plenty else though, none of it good. There was a pair that looked familiar, but I couldn't put a name to them. Then there was Curley Bill Morton, and a couple of his saddle bum companions sitting at a table near the windows on the street. Curley Bill was a bow-legged, runt of a man though not entirely bad-looking if it weren't for them black pig eyes of his. His dull, mousy brown hair hung straight, and in limp curls on his head. There was the look of a weasel about him. A dangerous weasel if I was any judge. His face was pinched and drawn like he hadn't eaten in a week. He looked to be one of the slimiest things to crawl out from under a rock for some time. The two with him were likely kin. Curley Bill had enough cousins and such to start their own town. I'd heard talk about his pa, Bull Morton, a time or two. It wasn't no secret why Curley's pa was called Bull. All a man had to do was take himself a good look.

When things slowed down some, Turk came up and put a fresh beer in front of me. He followed my gaze across the room to Morton's table and gave a low whistle.

'You know him, Matt?'

I shrugged. 'By sight, that's all.'

By the time I got those few words out of my mouth Curley Bill was up and heading our way. He moved with a swagger and slammed his empty whiskey bottle on the bar near hard enough to break it.

'Gimme a fresh one barkeep,' he ordered real nasty like. 'My friend and cousin over there are waiting with a powerful thirst.' He made a broad, slightly drunken gesture toward the table he'd just left.

It couldn't 'a been more plain, he was trouble-hunting as if he wore a sign. Me, I kept my attention on my beer, and waited for Turk to get his bottle, being in no mood to

8

go tangling with some little weasel who fancied himself with a gun.

'You ain't too friendly, are ya?' Curley Bill snapped as he turned toward me.

I looked at Turk. Seemed like I couldn't win. 'No,' I said quietly, 'I ain't,' hoping that would end it better'n some long explanation ... but like I said, seemed like I couldn't win.

'Sure as hell you ain't!' Curley exploded. 'I seen friendlier sidewinders.'

It was the whiskey talking. Leastways, I hoped that's what it was. I kept leaning up against the bar, keeping my horns pulled in.

'Hey,' he asked sullenly, 'you ignoring me?' He glanced toward the pair still at his table now looking in his direction. 'Nobody ignores Curley Bill Morton.' His voice was low, menacing.

'That's enough,' Turk put in, his voice low, matching Curley's. 'I'm not having any trouble here. You know what's under this bar, and it's pointing at your belly.'

Curley stared into Turk's gray eyes gone cold. Then, abruptly, he took his bottle and went back to his saddle partners.

'What's under there?' I asked, my curiosity up.

'Just a lil' old pea shooter,' Turk grinned as he brought his hands back on the top of the bar, a wet rag being the only thing he held.

'Like hell,' I said remembering the past, 'a
9

cannon's more likely.' For a moment I stood watching Curley Bill seat himself back at his table to finish his drink.

'You better watch him,' Turk said a mite more serious. 'That little snake is a lot more dangerous than he appears. He's a back-shooting son with no more respect for man nor woman than he has for a foul-smelling skunk.'

Just then something caught Turk's eye outside. He let his gaze slip past Curley's table to the window. 'We have something a lot better looking than that to look at in Tucson.' He nodded toward the window.

I glanced sideways at Turk, then looked out the window. Across the street, standing in front of the general store was a woman, and she was about the prettiest thing I'd laid eyes on in some time. I couldn't see her real good through the window and all, but she was small and moved with a quick step. She wore her thick, auburn hair loose, and the desert sun shone through it like it was satin. She was wearing one of them gray traveling outfits that were popular with womenfolks then, and she filled it out right nice. She was Eastern, that was plain enough to me.

'Real pretty, isn't she?' Turk chuckled.

Peering over the top of my beer glass I nodded. Nobody could argue with that. I could see Curley Bill was doing his own share of looking.

10

Turk leaned on the bar. 'I knew her father, Jack Tucker, real well, Matt. He knew this land as well as you do, my friend. Found himself a gold mine far back in the hills somewhere. There was no one around here would believe it. Some silver had been found, but no gold.'

Not knowing how reliable this here Jack Tucker was, I asked Turk. 'You sure it was the real thing?'

'Well, he showed me some of the stuff he brought back with him,' Turk said quickly, 'and it wasn't fool's gold, it was the real thing all right. He'd lived in the East for a long time and was tired of it. He told me the West had been his first love.'

'He have any special plans for that gold?' I asked, sipping my beer. Gold didn't hold any grip on me. All it bought folks was trouble and grief. I figured I had my share of that without adding to it.

'Well...' the way Turk was easing into this was beginning to make me nervous, 'when he found that gold, he planned to go back East to get his family. He had two sons and a daughter, staying with friends, waiting for him back there. His wife had been dead for eleven years.' Turk paused and looked at me. From the expression on his face, I knew he was working his way up to something. 'When he got back East he met with an unfortunate accident and was killed. His

11

sons came back here with a map, showing the way to the gold mine he'd found, with them. The older one, Sam, didn't know the desert, or the Indians. He brought his younger brother Jamie, and got himself tied up with a rawhide outfit to boot. That Jamie, he couldn't have been past eleven. Well, what happened was Sam got himself killed by the Apache and they took Jamie with them. There isn't any way of telling whether they kept the boy or killed him later.'

Me, I just shook my head. There wasn't no way to figure what a greenhorn would do next. Bringing an eleven-year-old boy out here wasn't exactly showing good sense, and I said as much. 'What was that Sam you mentioned using for brains, dried beans?'

Turk did his best to ignore my comment. 'I sent Ann Tucker, that pretty little girl over there, a wire when the Army brought back what was left of Sam. The captain with the patrol said Sam had a lot of sand. Took a couple of Apache with him when he went, which isn't an easy thing. Seemed to me someone ought to tell her what happened so's she wouldn't be wondering for the rest of her life what had become of her brothers. That's why she's here.'

'What do you mean that's why she's here?' I took me a long pull on my beer and met Turk's steady gaze.

'She's planning on going after her brother,

Jamie. She's looking for someone who'll scout for her.' He scratched his chin and kind of grinned sideways at me. 'I figured you not being with the Army any more you might consider...'

Well I mean to tell you, I choked and that beer flew out of my mouth like a fountain. I dragged the back of my hand across my mouth and eyed him for the crazy man I figured him to be.

'No,' I said shortly, and repeated it for effect. 'No!' Setting my beer glass on the bar, I just stared at him. 'Are you plumb loco? There's Indians out there, Apache, Cochise, Soldato, Natchez, and Victorio, to name a few. There ain't been any peace made that I know of. And she's figuring on looking for a little boy she ain't even sure is still alive?' I shook my head and hopped up on the bar dropping back to the other side. 'You ain't getting me into this, Turk,' I said loudly. 'I ain't taking no woman out into that.' I turned and started for the door. 'You tell that pretty little gal,' I said over my shoulder, 'to turn herself around and head herself back home. Ain't no man in his right mind gonna take her out into that desert. I'm gonna go get myself a bath and a shave,' I finished, and it seemed like every man in the place was a-starin' at me when I left, including Curley Bill and his crowd, them little pig eyes of his following me out the door ... and he was

13

smiling.

With long strides, I started across the street, clean forgetting about my horse tied in front of the saloon. I don't know where that Ann Tucker popped up from, but I near fell over her, I was moving that fast.

'Ma'am,' I said politely, touching my hatbrim to her.

She looked at me through soft brown eyes for a couple seconds, startled by the bump but didn't fall back as I passed by. She was still looking at me, a mite annoyed, when I remembered my horse and turned back for him. Close up, she was even more to look at than through a saloon window. She had that kind of skin that looked like it held the glow of an evening campfire. Her eyes were wide and round, the kind that could make some men feel weak in the knees, and if I'd a looked in 'em much longer, they'd 'a done it to me. Her nose was small and turned up some at the end with a few pale freckles not much darker in color than the desert sand, sprinkled across it. Her lips were sort of delicate and full, like they were painted on by a doll maker.

'Ma'am,' I repeated as I passed her a second time in the street to retrieve my horse.

That girl just stood there a-watchin' me, a smile that looked like sunrise spreading across her face, while I untied my horse and

14

started for the hotel again.

'Ma'am,' I said a third time, nodding to her, and went on into the hotel.

Looking a mite puzzled, she stood there looking after me kind of shaking her head, then turned and went on about her business.

I got me that hot bath and shave I was hunting, and a good night's sleep at the hotel. I rounded it off with a good breakfast of eggs, beef, potatoes, and several cups of strong black coffee. After what the Army had served up when I was in the fort, and the hardtack and jerky that was my fixin's while on the trail, that restaurant food tasted mighty good. There was no hurry in me this day. I had no place to be going and no business that needed tending.

I was a drifting man. Had been ever since I'd lost my wife some years back, though that wasn't the reason I hadn't settled down. Seemed like I'd just started drifting one day and hadn't stopped. Reckon I was kind of half looking for some place where folks weren't so hell-bent on flat out killing each other. I'd packed my share of trouble but I was longing for an end of it. Trouble wasn't something I went hunting but it seemed like it mostly was thrown on me, and then I just naturally settled things proper.

According to a calendar I'd seen behind the hotel desk, today was July third, and tomorrow was the day for all the celebrating.

15

A mighty long time had passed since I'd been in any kind of a town for some partying, and I was planning on hanging around.

Considerable time had passed me by since I'd sacked in late, and I'd even allowed myself that this morning. It was on past midmorning when I finished up breakfast and settled back in my chair to linger over my last cup of coffee a while longer. I liked watching folks passing by outside the restaurant and listening to their voices around me. After I'd been out in wild country for a spell, a town always looked good to me. Trouble was, I got tired of folks too quick and longed to head for open country again. It wasn't their fault though, it was mine. I just naturally felt more at home in the high places. Places where all a body saw was a few eagles, some mountain goats, and maybe a couple big cats.

When I glanced back up from my coffee I saw Turk angling his way across the street in my direction from the livery. He looked to me like a man who was mighty upset and had his mind set on something. Right off I got to worrying. I might'a considered ducking out of the restaurant, but he was looking me right in the eye and coming on fast. I didn't know what was up, but knowing Turk, it sure wouldn't be good. He come through that door like a charging bull, heading right for my table.

'I have to talk to you, Matt,' he said shortly. 'Where the devil you been all morning?'

Ignoring his question, I pushed a chair out from the table with one foot. 'Pull up a chair, Turk. Make yourself to home.'

He dropped into the offered chair. 'It's about that girl I was telling you about ... Ann Tucker.'

I sighed. 'Didn't you tell that girl to get on home?'

Turk looked helpless. 'More times than I can count, but she managed to find herself a scout anyway.'

Finishing my coffee I signaled for the girl to fill the cup again. 'Good for her, and I'm glad it wasn't me.'

Turk shook his head. His deeply lined face looked grim, his gray eyes worried. 'Not good at all, Matt. She got herself a rattlesnake. She hired on Curley Bill Morton and the pair that was with him in the saloon yesterday.'

Like a durned fool I just sat there and stared at him. 'Seems like that family is set on getting itself exterminated,' I said when I could finally get something out.

'Matt, I'm asking you to go after her. That Curley Bill is poison mean. There's no telling what he might do.'

'Well, he won't be riding out to no Apache camps, that much is sure.' All of a sudden I

17

was feeling kind of weary. Turk had me boxed in. He knew I owed him, and even if I didn't, I couldn't leave that little city gal out in the middle of the desert with the likes of Curley Bill and his bunch. Remembering those big, brown eyes of hers reminded me of my dead wife's eyes, so round and trusting. Pat had been alone when she caught the slug that killed her, just as Ann was alone now. It wasn't in me to leave her out there knowing she was with the likes of Curley Bill and knowing what they'd do to her. Turk'd figured once I knew she was alone out there I'd follow, and he was right. Well, there it was again. I hadn't even had time to pick the sand out from between my teeth from my scouting days and already I was fixing to head out again.

Now, I've lived in hard, wild country near all my life, and just 'cause I'd made up my mind to go after her, that didn't mean I was gonna run out the door, jump on my horse and ride. I knew a little about Curley Bill, and I didn't figure he'd be starting out at a walk. He'd be wanting to put a lot of country between him and the town right off, and they already had about half a day's start on me. I was gonna be needing me some supplies, water, and a couple of good guns.

I finished what was left of my coffee in a gulp. 'You still got that shotgun?' I asked Turk quickly.

18

He knew the one I meant, and he nodded. Turk had always kept it under the bar back in New Orleans. It was an odd sort of shotgun, kind of cut off at both ends. It was a revolver too, packing four shots. I had me a hide-out gun in my bedroll as well. A .44 derringer. A man couldn't be too careful when he was fixing to head into the kind of country I was figuring on. The Apache were there, that much was for sure, but they weren't alone. Banditos from Mexico often crossed through the desert as did the Comancheros. Then, there were the likes of Curley Bill Morton, and he wasn't alone. I could not be called a cautious man, for caution was something I used only rarely. I was only ready, ready for what I knew waited for me out there alone. And ready to kill, not because I liked killing, but because I knew there were those who would kill me. Life is a lot like a poker game. Bid, bluff, and call. When a man was called, it paid to be holding all the high cards.

The girl who was waiting tables headed back in my direction. 'He'll pay the bill,' I gestured toward Turk. I picked up my hat and settled it firmly on my head. 'If you don't see me again, I think you'd better figure that debt of mine paid.' I grinned and went out to put myself together an outfit.

CHAPTER TWO

Ann Tucker was determined. Determined to find Jamie, the only one of her family who was left. Others had doubts, but she knew inside he wasn't dead. Actually, it wasn't altogether true that Jamie was the only one of her family still alive. There was an uncle she hadn't even mentioned to Turk, a cruel and ornery man. She'd never had any use for the man. Neither had her father, and they'd been brothers.

Jamie was different, he was more like her son than her brother. Their mother had died when he was born. Ann hadn't been much past eleven herself then, but she'd taken care of Jamie, brought him up. She figured he'd be expecting her to come after him.

While she had her mind set on what she was doing, and wasn't about to turn back, neither was she a fool. Turk saw her before she rode out, though only for a minute. She left town wearing man's clothes. Shirt, pants, boots, hat, and a shapeless poncho to help protect her from the desert sun. All told, her appearance was considerably different from the night before, and she rode with an assurance that showed years of experience. All the years she was growing up she had listened to her father's stories about the

Western lands and she had also picked up know-how and savvy along the way.

There was a rifle in the saddle scabbard beside her knee. She knew what she'd hired in Curley Bill and his companions, but there'd been no others, and it wasn't in her to turn back. She didn't put any trust in him, but he seemed peaceable enough as he rode beside her. And they were making very good time, better than she'd hoped. Still, it wasn't wise to trust a rattlesnake just because it hadn't bitten you yet.

It was hot. Ann had a habit of looking around real good. Far in the distance the mountains looked cool and beckoning. During the years when he'd been home, her father had talked many hours of the desert. Of the things that grew there, and the men that walked the land. Many times he talked about the land itself, rough and merciless. The blazing sun burning overhead, parching the earth, and then there were the hot winds that seemed to sweep across the land without ever letting up. She'd figured she knew what to expect, but hearing was never the same as experiencing.

They'd started out in the coolness before dawn, but that hadn't lasted long once the sun started climbing in the sky. Southeast out of Tucson was where they were headed, right into the heart of Apache territory. Fortunately for her she'd spent enough time

21

roaming in the woods back home to know if they stuck to their true direction.

Ann was mindful of cover, surprisingly so for a city gal, for that had been one thing her father had spoken on very strongly. He'd told her a man had to ride desert country knowing there were always eyes on him, knowing that at any minute the Apache could come right up out of the desert. A man caught in the open was as good as dead he'd told her. Her father spoke of the Apache with the greatest respect. They were fighting to keep their land. It was war. It had been as simple as that. From a long-range viewpoint, she'd always agreed with her father, but now they had Jamie, and that was some different. It wasn't that she felt the need for revenge, but she wouldn't rest easy until she had Jamie safely back with her either. As she rode there wasn't much, some scrub brush, prickly pear, and the giant saguaros whose green arms reached as high as fifty feet into the sky. A few hollows, and some dry washes that could be used for shelter of sorts if need be were passed by. It seemed to her that they were about as secure as they could be in Apache country, but she was nervous. What she felt was some kind of inner warning, and she listened real good.

They stopped when the sun was almost directly overhead, at a place where the rocks and cactus clustered around each other in a rough half circle topping the edge of an old dry wash. It provided shelter and shade, both of which were more than welcome as far as Ann was concerned. Before Curley Bill had the chance to pull his chivalrous act and help her, she slid down off her horse. Having him put a hand on her, for any reason, was something that made her hair stand on end. She tended her horse, ate her cold lunch of jerky and bread, and kept her rifle close at hand. It was partly out of respect for the closeness of the Indians, and mostly because of Curley Bill and the two riding with him, Jed Sloan and Abel Jenkins. She hadn't figured on hiring three men, and it was kind of funny how they showed up all of a sudden wanting to leave right away, but no one else would go. Curley Bill had flatly refused to hit the trail without his cousin and friend. Back in town it hadn't seemed such a bad idea to her. It had even seemed it would be a little safer with three guns besides her own, and Curley Bill had even seen to all the details about supplies. But out here there was a difference. The way they looked at her and the way they treated her was beginning to make her more than a mite edgy. The change started almost as soon as they'd left Tucson behind. It was made plain to her that she was a woman alone, and that they figured her for carrying a lot of money. In Tucson they would have been right, but she had left every

23

penny behind in the bank. She had told them that, and they had all grinned and nodded, but had they really believed her? She had to sleep some time, Ann wasn't fool enough to think different, and she was sure that was when Curley Bill would make his move. Turning back while it was still this early, giving her plenty of time to reach Tucson before dark crossed her mind. But, she figured it'd all just happen again. She wasn't going to quit trying to go after Jamie. She was more determined than a wolverine taking on a full-growed mountain lion. It crossed her mind that she was going to have to give the matter some careful thought, and that she'd better come up with something by the time they set up camp for the night.

Staring across their little camp and eating, Ann sat on a large rock, her rifle resting across her bent knee when Curley got up and started toward her. Warily, she followed his coming across the few feet of sand with her eyes. Tipping his hat back on his head a bit he gave her one of his slimy-looking grins.

'We're heading southeast, just like you said, ma'am.' Curley Bill propped one boot on a rock beside Ann. 'Heading right into Injun land.'

Ann nodded. 'I know. I've been watching.' She allowed herself one swallow of water to wash down the jerky and bread, then turned her attention to Curley. 'The Flying L is that way,' she added, pointing almost due east. 'We should get there late tomorrow.'

'That would take us outa' our way, ma'am. Ain't no reason to stop off at the Flannigan spread.' Curley looked a little unhappy as he spoke. He wasn't the sort to want to risk any complications.

Ann shook her head. She was figuring, trying to give herself some small edge, anything that might head off trouble. 'You're wrong, there's a good reason. I promised Turk I'd send him word from the Flying L that I'd gotten that far safely.'

She was not mistaken. A look of surprised anger flashed across Curley's face. She hadn't promised Turk any such thing when she left Tucson, but she was plenty glad she'd said it. It would give Curley a little something extra to think about.

Curley Bill tightened his lips and frowned. 'All right ma'am, the Flying L it is. You're doing the paying. We'll be pulling outa' here in just a few minutes.' He turned and went on back to where his cousin Abel was standing with the horses. Jed was up in the rocks somewhere standing watch.

It worried Ann some that Curley went off a distance and talked with Abel so's she couldn't hear them, and she had a right to be worried.

'Says she told that barkeep back in Tucson she'd send word from Flannigan's spread

25

that she's all right,' Curley told Abel a mite nervously. 'Think we ought to put things off for a few day, maybe?'

'Hell,' Abel scoffed, 'earliest word that could get back to Tucson is four days. Lot can happen in four days. 'Sides,' he added in a worried voice, 'the longer we wait, the further we get into Apache land. Seems to me we're already risking our necks an awful lot just waiting for tonight. If that man hadn't offered you so much money, I'd 'a told you it wasn't worth the risk.'

'Guess you're right.' Curley glanced up toward the rocks where Jed was keeping watch. 'Come on down, we're pulling out.'

They pushed on until almost sundown, Ann naturally riding in the lead with Curley Bill. Finally, they stopped in a little hollow where rocks rose steeply on one side giving them a good lookout, and brush sort of ringed two more sides which helped hide their camp. The horses were staked inside the camp circle where they could be watched, and this time there was a small fire. The sticks were very dry and gave off no smoke to give away their camping place.

The sky was still holding the fiery glow of sunset when Ann put up some coffee and made a warm broth out of some jerky for herself. They'd packed plenty of food with them. There was jerky, hardtack, plenty of beans, and some salt pork. It wouldn't have

26

set a fancy table, but after a long day on a rough trail it didn't matter much what the grub looked like, or even what it tasted like, so long as it filled the empty feeling in a man's stomach.

After they'd eaten, Ann sat back a ways from the fire. Glancing up as Abel Jenkins passed by her to stand watch up in the rocks, Ann caught him openly leering in her direction. She'd thought of nothing during their day of riding that would let her sidestep trouble that might be coming. There wasn't much anyone could do in such a situation. The Mortons lived off trouble, that was a fact. Curley and Abel were cousins. Anything Abel was planning on, Curley was a part of, that was for certain. Ann couldn't figure Jed Sloan. He was a different matter. Inoffensive in appearance, with reddish-brown hair and watery brown eyes, he looked like a bank clerk. There was something about him though, whenever he got near, Ann could feel the flesh along her neck turn cold. Mostly, he just sat quiet, a little apart from Curley, picking at his fingernails with a knife.

When Ann looked over at Curley Bill, his small black eyes were a'boring through her, and in that second she knew they had never planned on letting her live through the first night. She felt a flash of panic staring into Curley's calm taunting face. An almost uncontrollable urge to run swept over her, but reason had always been with her, and it didn't leave her cold now. She'd worked herself into a pretty good corner and all she could do was be ready. In her situation, there was little else anyone could a'done.

Calmly, showing no fear, Ann dragged her saddle over between some rocks and started laying out her bedroll. She felt sick to her stomach and her hands were shaking, but the action drew no more than a casual glance from Curley. What they were waiting for, Ann didn't know, but all she needed was a few more minutes to be about as ready as she could get. The place where she'd laid her bedroll was tight up between a pair of large rocks. The shadows hid her movements, and made it impossible for more than one of the three to come at her at one time. She settled down on her bedroll and laid quiet, letting Curley and Jed get used to the idea of her drifting off to sleep. Sleep though, was one thing she wasn't counting on. When she saw Curley look away, she began easing her hand up toward her rifle which was still on her saddle. Curley was talking with Jed in low, inaudible tones. Ann was feeling wound tight as a bedspring. Her hand touched the smooth wooden stock of the rifle and she started easing it out of the scabbard. It slid easily from the leather. Keeping the barrel low to the ground so as it wouldn't catch and reflect the light from the campfire, Ann slid the rifle under her blanket. She closed her eyes for a second and let out a long, quiet sigh. Her mind was in a fog, but she was still thinking. She was scared silly but all her father had told her hadn't prepared her for this. She wished he was with her. All her life she'd never been afraid when he was near. Over and over in her mind she called his name, knowing this was one time he wouldn't answer. Carefully, after letting her jumping nerves have a chance to settle, she eased herself into a more upright position, her back against the saddle. The butt end of her rifle was braced against the ground, the barrel leaning up against her leg, and her hand resting on the trigger. Ann watched the fire dying out and heard the horses stamp a little way off. A few more words passed between Curley Bill and Jed, then Curley stood up, stretched, and started toward her. She felt her heart jump up into her throat, but her hand remained dry where she gripped the rifle. Fear filled the air around her like a living thing. She knew they were counting on her being asleep and she hoped that this should give her an edge she desperately needed. Curley crossed those last few feet of desert sand as she watched in silence, the pounding of her heart seeming so loud she was sure he must hear it.

'You want something, Curley?' Ann asked

as he came up in front of her.

Curley stopped short. 'I thought you were asleep.' Then after a short pause he said, 'I think you know what I want!'

Ann shook her head. 'Sorry, Curley, I don't know. Why don't you tell me?' Ann never could figure how she managed to keep her voice calm when inside she was screaming.

The whole thing was making Curley Bill nervous, she just wasn't acting like he expected. And when he got nervous he tended to talk too much. 'You know we got to kill you,' he said like he was commenting on the clearness of the night sky. 'But if you're real nice to me, I'll make it fast. You won't hardly feel a thing. Or maybe,' he smirked, 'we could even leave you in some little town somewheres and nobody would ever have to see you again.' That last part was a lie, and Ann wasn't fool enough to think different.

'Kill me? I told you before, Curley, I left all my money in Tucson. What would you get by killing me?' Ann could feel herself shaking.

Curley was inching his way forward. 'We're getting a real good price for you.' He completely blocked the light from the campfire, so Ann couldn't see his face, but she knew he'd be grinning. Seemed like he never stopped grinning.

'That's a good offer you made me, Curley. Might even consider taking you up on it if I didn't have this rifle aimed right at your middle.' She forced the words out strong and sure, but inside she was whimpering, praying for something, anything to change what was happening.

The tone in her voice brought Curley up short, but then he came on, still inching his way forward. 'Ol' Curley Bill' hadn't learned his lesson about coming up on a loaded gun. It wasn't a sensible thing to do. 'I don't believe you,' he chuckled softly. 'You're real smart though, trying a bluff on me.'

'You better believe it, Curley.' Ann raised the rifle a bit to keep him covered. She didn't want to pull that trigger, she couldn't even know what was gonna happen for sure, she'd never seen it, but she held death in her hands, and it wasn't an easy burden.

Even in the dim blackness between the rocks Curley caught the flicker of motion to her right, and he grabbed for it. More through reflex than thought, Ann pulled the trigger. The rifle exploded. The shot split the air, the sound of it contained between the rocks, slamming against her ears. The kick of the gun against the ground sent a jolt traveling all the way up her arm to her shoulder. Curley stumbled back a couple of feet and fell to the ground, dead. Jed jumped to his feet, his gun out. He took one look at

31

Curley Bill and aimed his gun at the dim lump between the rocks that was Ann. Almost without thinking, the smell of gunpowder still filling her nose, Ann shifted her aim to cover Jed when Curley went down. Then she had no choice, and her father's words were ringing in her ears as if it were only yesterday when she'd first heard them spoken. Always, he'd told Sam, in the Western lands a man didn't pull a gun unless he aimed to shoot ... and he didn't shoot unless he aimed to kill. Ann had listened good, and now she was learning.

She didn't want to kill again, but she was cornered. For only an instant she'd paused, and it almost cost her her life. Jed had no intention of risking her rifle, and would have killed her from where he stood if she hadn't pulled the trigger that second time. Jed's Colt went off at the same instant as Ann's rifle. The bullet slammed into a rock with a sharp, cracking whine and whipped past her head as Jed was thrown back beside what was left of the campfire.

'Are you crazy?' Abel's voice reached her before she saw him. 'The Apache'll hear them shots for miles...' Seeing both Jed and Curley laying in the sand, Abel pulled up short, not quite sure where to turn. He had a rifle in his hands, but he wasn't figuring on using it.

'Just don't move, Abel,' Ann said sharply,

surprised at the force of her own voice. Behind the shielding dimness of the shadows she was trembling from head to where the soles of her boots touched the sand, the sweat springing out across her face despite the coolness of the night air. 'I just killed two men, it wouldn't take much for me to make it three.' She felt all out of breath like she'd just run uphill a ways. 'I have a rifle, and I guess there's enough proof now for you at least to believe me.'

Abel was standing there kind of wide-eyed, not moving just like she said. 'You got a rifle all right, ain't no question about that,' he blurted out.

'All right,' Ann could feel the tightness in her chest, the dryness in her throat, but she managed to keep her voice steady. 'Then I suggest you drop yours. Your gunbelt too,' she gestured toward his middle when he threw down the rifle. 'Then, you climb up on your horse and ride out, and don't let me see you looking back.'

'But this is Apache country,' Abel whined. 'Them shots are gonna bring 'em all a-runnin'. You gotta let me have a gun.'

'Get on your horse and ride out,' Ann repeated. Her source of strength was not a bottomless well, and she could feel what was left of it starting to drain away.

Abel cursed under his breath, but he didn't argue with a rifle pointing at him. He got his horse saddled up and cleared out.

Ann watched him go, then looked back at Jed and Curley Bill, and almost lost her supper. Somehow she forced her stomach back into place. She couldn't even afford herself the luxury of being sick. Swiftly, blocking her mind to the two dead men within the camp's circle, Ann saddled her horse and the better one of the other two. That was Curley's horse, a sandy colored animal that looked like he was built for speed as well as for distance. With two mounts, she was counting on being able to change off, saving them both for a time when she might have to run. She split the food and water between the two horses, and gathered up the weapons, including the side arms from Curley Bill and Jed. Touching the dead men made her feel weak in the knees, and it was only the thinking of Jamie that gave her the strength to do what had to be done. She strapped on Abel's sidegun to have close at hand. In one thing, Abel had been right. The Apache would be heading in this direction to investigate the shots.

As much a part of the desert as any animal living there, and fighting for survival, Ann was alone. She turned Jed's horse loose and tied Curley's heavy jacket on the back of her own horse. A time might come when she would need it. With one last quick look around, she snuffed out the campfire and mounted up. The saddle creaked as it took her weight. Ann thanked whatever luck or fate it was that made this a night with a full moon. The night was clear and cold, the horse beneath her seemed eager for the trail. Her first thought had been to stay on her chosen route, but when she put her horse to the trail, she changed her mind and cut off some to the north.

By daybreak Ann knew she'd have to be finding a sheltered camp. She knew the horses would need rest, and so, too, would she. But just as important was laying low and keeping out of the way of the Apache. There was a lot of thinking she had to do. If she had an ounce of sense she would try to swing around and cut back for Tucson. Unfortunately, being sensible wasn't something Ann had very often been accused of.

CHAPTER THREE

That roan horse of mine was all mustang. Seemed like he was raring to go any hour of the day or night. He lit out of Tucson like his tail was afire and he was glad to be heading for open country again. A lot of desert was covered by him and me by sundown, but it wasn't enough to close the lead Curley Bill and his little troupe had on us. It kind of figured that way from the start, and when the sun went down I had me a good case of the worries. Something was gonna happen the first night out, I could feel it in my bones. Curley Bill and that pair with him wouldn't head right into Apache land ... they didn't have the stomach for it.

I wasn't figuring on camping at all for the night. I just climbed down off'a my horse in an old dry wash, giving him a breather while I bolted down some food to keep my stomach from biting my backbone and maybe growling at the wrong time. I gave my horse a little water and had one foot back in the stirrup when I heard them shots. They were a long ways off, but sound carries far in the quiet of a desert night. There was one shot, then two more close together. Sounded like a rifle, and maybe a handgun, but I couldn't be sure of the handgun, the last two shots being so close together. The shots had come more from the east than the south of me but it couldn't have been any others. It had to be Ann Tucker and the three with her. Every time I thought of that pretty little gal, her auburn hair a-shinin' in the sun like I saw her back in town, it gave me a chill to think of her alone in the desert with the likes of Curley Bill and his lot.

When I lit out in the direction of the shots, I was flat out expecting to find little Ann

Tucker dead, give her a decent burial, and head back for town at a run before I lost my hair. Thing was, that wasn't the way I found it at all.

It had been fairly easy for me to locate the camp. It was hidden some, but Curley Bill had been no expert. A few tracks and a little figuring brought me right to it. When I found Curley Bill and Jed Sloan a-layin' there in the sand dead, a body could've knocked me over with a cross-eyed look. They were both stone, cold dead, and both shot through with a rifle from the looks of things. At first I figured it for Indians, but when I got to looking things over I found out different. I could see where one horse had been turned loose, another rode off to the northwest carrying a heavy load, and a pair went off almost due east, edging a little north. The pair of horses were both traveling light. Since there was no trace of the girl in camp, and small bootprints showed where the horses had been, that had to be Ann. I did me some fast checking, and what I came up with didn't make sense. It was right there in front of me, but it was downright hard to swallow. That pert little girl I'd seen on the streets in Tucson had killed two men. Looked like Curley Bill had made the mistake of coming after her after she'd bedded down and caught a rifle slug right through the heart for his trouble. Jed had fared no better. That girl had uncanny luck, or she knew how to handle a rifle. What bothered me was the set of tracks leading off to the northeast. She'd let one go, and from the evidence laying at my feet, that one had to have been Abel Jenkins. Ann Tucker looked to have her a lot of sand, but she wasn't showing good sense in letting that one go. Still, she'd have no way of knowing what kind of trouble he could bring her.

I'd pushed my horse pretty hard to get here, and he needed a breather, so I buried the two men by caving in some dirt from the loose edge of the hollow and piling some rocks on top.

I wasn't a man to do much worrying most times. Usually, I just took things as they came, but this here was something different. From the tracks I'd found, that girl was heading deeper into Apache territory all the time. Indians were all around here, and that was bad enough, but she was heading right into their strongholds. It entered my mind that maybe she had some brains loose. Seemed to me, any woman in her right mind, who just went through what she had and lived, would be eager to get herself on back to some kind of civilization.

Well, there wasn't much else I could do except follow her. There was my promise to Turk, and then there was always the chance she just couldn't figure direction right and picked the wrong way. From what I'd seen here though, I had my doubts that that was true. The tracks set out sure and straight, they didn't wander none.

Up on my roan again, we started out right smart, but tracking at night is a tricky thing, even with a full moon. It unsettled me some, but I couldn't let her get too big a lead on me, and to top it off, I knew them Apache would be closing in on that camp to see about them shots just as I had. And all the time, a corner of my mind was a-hangin' on Abel Jenkins. Abel had been Curley Bill's cousin. Ol' Curley Bill, he had him lots of kin. Abel, he was a fidgeter, a coat holder, a man who talked a good fight, but wanted no part of one. But he would certainly be of a mind to let the rest of Curley's kin know what happened as soon as he could reach a town. Now Curley Bill and his kinfolks weren't never kindly disposed toward folks anyhow, but when they found out Curley Bill had been fetched up, and by a woman, there'd be hell to pay. There was enough to be tugging at a man's mind out here with them Apache all over the place without giving thought to what was gonna happen when he got back to town. Trouble was, I didn't have much choice. I'd heard tell a lot about Bull Morton. For danged sure he would be waiting in Tucson, if I managed to get that girl back there in one piece.

Following what trail I could find, I took me two wrong turns in the dark before I took to cussin' Turk Billings for getting me into this. When I picked up the trail again it was just a short spell 'til dawn. I climbed down again to let my horse rest and wait for dawn, figuring to make up some time with daylight. At least during the early morning hours I could move fast. After that, the heat would slow me down again. The trail seemed to be heading more east than south, even drifting a hair north. If she kept on going, that would take her up to the Flannigan spread. Could be she figured it was closer than town and lit out for there after her trouble. It was a comforting thought, but not a very convincing one.

A sliver of sun was barely creeping up past the eastern horizon when I took out again. It seemed to me that she had to be moving pretty good herself to keep up ahead of me like she was. That had to mean she wasn't being too cautious about the Apache. Somebody must have told her that story about them not fighting at night. It was true to a point, but they made exceptions, and I had a sneaky hunch a woman alone would be one of them.

It was getting on to midmorning when I found the fresh tracks. I mean, they couldn't have been more'n an hour old. She had to have stopped to rest for quite a spell for me to catch up like that. It wasn't that I weren't thankful, coming up on her so quick, it's just that them tracks led off into what looked to me to be a box canyon. Now, it might be a box canyon with only one way in or out, or it might be that it had a back way into the hills. It was the not knowing that made a man right jumpy. That roan of mine was a good desert horse, and he smelled water. Well, there wasn't no getting around it, I was going up that canyon. I gave a last look around the countryside before I started down the canyon opening. I didn't really expect to see anything, and I wasn't disappointed.

Going up that canyon quiet as an Injun, I stuck to the soft sand and such. I didn't want to spook that little gal, bein' as how I was so close to her. She was apt to be mighty nervous and wary of strangers. Soon as I got myself well within the canyon, I tied my horse in the thick of some chaparral and went ahead on foot carrying my Winchester with me. I kept that rifle close 'cause I just plain didn't want to be separated from it in this country. I was thinking about the 'Pache too. They could be all around this canyon, and neither the girl or I would know a thing about it 'til they were ready to let us in on it.

A steep trail led off to one side of the canyon, looking like it went straight up to the top. It was that trail the two horses I was tracking took. My horse could have followed

41

easily, but I preferred going on foot. There had been a lot of mesquite below, but it thinned out considerable as I went higher. Mostly, there was just cactus, a few of the giants and a lot of the low stuff a man had to keep his eye on to keep from getting himself cut up. The sand and rock was loose underfoot.

I topped out on the lip of a bowl-shaped cut in the hillside where the gentle slope upward was backed by a sheer rock cliff. A small rock tank on the far side, not much bigger'n a washbasin, caught the water as it dribbled from a seep and held it.

Two horses were standing quiet like off to one side. They looked to have been watered and cared for. Ann was lying flat on her stomach, drinking deep from the little pool. Her hair was done up under a broad-brimmed hat, she was wearing man's clothes, and a gun that I was willing to bet had belonged to one of Curley Bill's bunch, but there was no mistaking her. She'd had a lot of luck, and Lord knows, probably some kind of guardian angel a-lookin' out for her to get her this far. Thing was, she was smart too. She was smart, quick to learn, and took to the desert like it was second nature to her. I'd never come across a woman before who took to the desert like her. Most women knew the ways of a city, a little house in a small town somewheres or the like, but left

42

alone out in the sand and cactus, they wouldn't last as long as a snowflake in July.

I was hunkered down on the edge of that bowl, not more'n twenty feet away from her, trying to figure how to come up on her, giving her the least start, when I saw something stir in the sand beyond her on her right. It took me a few seconds to get a good look at what it was, but when I did I stood up like I'd lit on a cactus. It was a damned sidewinder! Just a little earlier he'd been curled up in the shade of a rock, but the sun had moved and was forcing him to search for a cooler place to wait out the day. That snake couldn't have been more'n a foot away from Ann's hand, and that was the only direction he could take. Me, I was sweating. Sidewinders have been known to have a nasty habit of striking without warning. All I needed now was to be stuck out here with a snake-bit girl.

Well, I had me a choice. Either leave things alone and hope the snake just passed her by, which he might do if she didn't scream or jump. Or, I could say something and risk her jumping. Or, I could just shoot the snake, hope to kill it clean, and give that girl the scare of her life.

Never had been one for taking things slow. Hitting that pretty gal instead of the snake was a possibility, but I didn't reckon I had a choice but to try. I was sweating some, but I wasn't one to worry much on something that hadn't happened ... so, I took me a real careful aim, and just up and shot the snake. Well, I hit him square just as he was fixing to move and he just sort of folded up across the trigger guard of her rifle. Ann grabbed for that rifle when she heard my shot, the sound of it still echoing through the hills, but she pulled up short when she saw that snake and grabbed for the gun in holster. Probably figured on seeing Apache up on the slope when she turned, but all she saw was me. I came down the steep little trail toward her real slow, my rifle barrel pointing toward the sky.

'That's far enough.' She had that six-gun centered somewheres around my belt buckle when she asked, 'Who are you?' She was looking mighty jumpy, and I reckon she had a right.

I stopped where I was just like she said, and grinned. 'I'm the man who just kilt that snake.' It seemed to me a good time to remind her I'd just done her a favor. 'Name's Matt Logan.'

'Well, Mr Logan,' she said real slow like. 'I'm new out here, and alone, but I'm learning fast, so just keep your distance.' She glanced around at the snake and frowned. Then, more to herself than to me, she started talking. 'I didn't hear it rattle. I thought it was supposed to rattle before it would strike.'

'That was your first mistake, ma'am,' I said grinning a little. 'Sidewinders, sometimes they like to get sneaky and strike without warning a body. Now, your second mistake was telling me you're all alone out here. That kind of thing can put ideas in a man's head that weren't there before, long as he was expecting another man to be showing up at any minute.' I wiped my sleeve across my forehead. It was sure building up to a hot one. 'Your third mistake,' I continued lightly, 'was pointing that thing at my belt buckle.' I gestured toward the gun. 'If you're planning on shooting a man, you better shoot to kill, 'cause if he ain't dead on the first shot, he just might take it into his head to take you along with him. Gutshot, that's a hard way to go, and a man might have considerable time before he quit this world.' I couldn't help teasing a mite. This was no country for a woman. And, though I made light of it, this country was packed full of trouble.

Ann Tucker sat there by the edge of the pool, staring at me. Her face, burned lightly by the desert sun to a faint pink, was a mixture of surprise, anger, and puzzlement. My words of teasing sure hadn't done much to sooth her ruffled feathers. 'Why are you out here following me?' she asked, a mite peevish, 'and don't try to tell me you

45

weren't,' she added quickly.

'I never figured on lying to you, Miss Tucker,' I told her more serious like, then shrugged. 'Turk Billings asked me to come after you soon as he heard you hired on Curley Bill and his outfit. He wants me to bring you back to Tucson. Said something to me before I left about bringing you back no matter what I had to do to get the job done.'

Her face softened some, and she gave a little laugh. 'Turk must really have something on you for you to come running all the way out here in the thick of the Apache on his say so.' She shook her head. 'Turk likes to play substitute father, but I'm not going back to Tucson ... at least, not yet.'

I took off that old battered hat I wore and resettled it on my head. 'A woman don't belong out here, ma'am, and you're gonna have to forgive me for putting it this way ... Turk said he wanted you safe in town no matter how I had to do it, including hog-tying you and dragging you back.'

If Ann was surprised at what I'd just said, she sure didn't show it. She just looked at me calmly and nodded. 'You could do that,' she admitted. 'But,' she added, 'you'd have to watch me every minute after you did. If I got a chance, I'd slip away. And even if you got me all the way back to Tucson, I'd take the first horse I could lay my hands on and start

46

again, so what good would you have done?'

Much as I hated to admit it, she had a point, and all this talk was making me nervous. 'Ma'am, I hate to hurt you, but your little brother Jamie is probably already dead. And if he ain't, them 'Pache might 'a took him all the way down into Mexico by now. How you figuring on finding him?'

'Jamie is not dead,' she stated flatly, 'and as for finding him, I'll manage.'

Rubbing a hand over my face, I frowned. It was plumb loco, and I knew it. Seemed like I was always picking up strays, and Lord how she reminded me of my wife Pat who'd been killed by that stray bullet some years back. If I had any sense at all, I'd drag her back like Turk said, and clear out before anything else could happen. Trouble was, she was headstrong and determined. It was plain to me, she didn't figure to do any different than she said. If she did slip away from me we'd be running in circles on this desert, and that wasn't a risk worth taking. Pat would'a been the same, and I couldn't 'a left her either. Looked like I was heading through Injun country, either with Ann or trailing along behind.

'All right,' I said slowly, 'you ain't goin' back to Tucson. Looks like I ain't neither.' The words were out, there wasn't no backing down.

She gave me a long look, like them big

brown eyes of hers were looking right through me. Then she just up and put the gun back in her holster that was hanging from her oversized belt. It's not that I was complaining, not having that thing pointed at my belly, it just sort of took me by surprise was all. She picked up her rifle by its barrel, and gingerly slid the dead snake off the stock before slipping it into the saddleboot.

Well, there I was a-standin' with my mouth hanging open. I was gonna say something, but thought better of it and figured to let things stand as they were.

'We best get fixed for high ridin', Miss Tucker,' I finally said to her. 'With all this shootin' the past day or so, the 'Pache are sure out looking for something by now.'

She nodded and gathered up her horses' reins. 'You better call me Ann,' she advised as she come up alongside me. 'Miss Tucker is fine for the parlor, or some dance.'

That was how we started out, her and me, heading off the trail into the desert country where not many white men had passed before. It was a chancy thing, leaving a trail in the desert, but I'd been scouting that country long as I could remember, and I knew the waterholes. The Apache knew there was something going on by now, but they didn't know exactly where we were, at least that was how it seemed to me. If they spotted us before we found Jamie, the only thing left to do was run like hell and pray, 'cause odds were we wouldn't make it out.

CHAPTER FOUR

A tall, slender man stepped off the westbound stage at Tucson. He wore no hat, and his thick black hair was sweat-soaked and limp. His dark brown eyes held a cold light as he glanced around the town. It was plain he wasn't happy with what he saw. The dusty little desert town was far from the style of living to which he was accustomed. The heavy carpetbag the driver threw down to him he caught with ease, but there was a look of disgust on his handsome features. He swore under his breath. As soon as he got what he had come for in this Godforsaken place he figured to go back East and never give another thought to this dry, dusty land.

The clerk up at the hotel smiled real friendly like as the stranger came inside, but the smile was not returned. Wordlessly, the stranger signed the register with a flourish and continued brushing the dust from his ordinarily immaculate Eastern suit. His face was hard, grimly set, the lines deep. Though his skin was naturally dark, a body could see it wasn't near as dark as that of the Westerners who lived beneath the desert sun.

The clerk turned the register. He tried once more to be friendly. 'Glad to have you with us, Mr Tucker.' Taking a key from the board behind him, he handed it across the desk to the well-dressed stranger. 'Room's at the head of the stairs to your left.'

Adam Tucker muttered his thanks. Taking the key the clerk held out, he went on up the stairs, with long, fast strides, out of sight from the clerk.

Once again, the clerk read the name on the register in front of him, a mite puzzled. That book was getting mighty thick with Tuckers. First, there'd been Jack. He'd been some older than the one who'd just checked in, but he was Western, a man could see it in the way he carried himself. Then, there had been the two boys, Sam and the younger one Jamie. They'd only stayed a night. He had been real sorry to hear about Sam being killed and Jamie being taken by the Apache. Finally, there'd been that girl, and she had ridden off with a mighty mean outfit. From what he'd been able to get out of Turk, that scout, what was his name? ... Logan. He was trailing along behind. To his way of thinking, there wasn't too much hope for that girl. And now there was this one. Adam Tucker. Could be he was kin too. Charlie Harper had spent a lot of years behind a hotel desk, and he'd seen a lot of men come and go. Some in pine boxes. If Adam Tucker hadn't been an Easterner, Charlie would have figured him for a gunslick. There was something about them dark brown eyes, something kind of cold-looking, and a mite cruel. It was hard to think of him as being kin to that little slip of a thing out in the desert somewhere. Charlie sat back with a shrug. He wasn't going nowhere. Sooner or later he was sure to hear what was going on.

While Charlie was doing all that thinking, Adam Tucker was closing the door to his room behind him, and dropping his dusty carpetbag on the floor just inside the door. Sand sifted down and settled on the floor around it. The room was what he had expected to find in a town this size. It was small and dark with only a bed, washstand, and wardrobe. Dingy, sun-rotted curtains hung by the windows. It was near impossible to tell what color they'd once been. The room did overlook the street, which was about the only good thing about it. Adam Tucker shed his topcoat, throwing it on the bed, then took off his shirt so's he could wash some of the Western dust from his skin. Around his neck a small leather pouch was hanging from a leather thong. It had been made from a map of the southern part of the Arizona Territory. Naturally, the markings were turned to the inside. It was the map his brother had been carrying when

51

he'd been killed in that accident back East. From the instant Adam had realized the value of the map his brother was carrying, he knew he had to have it. He had never done too well back in New York, and his expensive way of life kept him in debt. The map was Adam's ticket to his brother's gold mine.

Jack Tucker and his brother Adam had been down by the waterfront together. One of the heavy boxes stacked on the docks had somehow been stacked off balance and chose the exact moment that Jack was passing to fall. It had been a lucky, freak accident, as far as Adam was concerned, because he had already been trying to figure out some way of getting his hands on that map without throwing suspicion on himself. Likely, he'd felt a twinge at his brother's death, but there wasn't no way he could bring him back ... and he had the map.

While Adam was washing himself, he thought of Sam who had all but committed suicide, going out into Indian territory like he had. Dragging Jamie with him to be taken by the Apache hadn't been very smart either. He hadn't known about the second map in Sam's possession when he'd taken the map from Jack's body. In all honesty, he'd a had to admit he wouldn't have wanted to tangle with Sam. A hot-headed young man like Sam would have been even more of a handful than Jack. For a short time, Adam's plans had died. Then the news about Sam and Jamie came across the wire. There'd been a time when family had meant something to him. Along the way somewheres, that'd died, and all that was left was a burning need for money. The need for more of it than anyone else had. He'd gone through the motions of pretending to comfort his niece even though he knew she'd never cared one whit for him. But the whole time he was going ahead with his plans to find the mine. To his way of thinking, there would be no one to stop him.

He had already been ready to leave town when word reached him that Ann was going after Jamie. But he knew better than that. She was going after that gold her father had left just the same as he. It had made him mad as a wet hen to think of his little niece acting so noble when all the time he knew it was the gold she was after. There must have been a third map. No matter which way he turned, more and more problems arose. The only way out for him, the only way for the gold to be his with no questions was for Ann to be dead. It hadn't been an easy decision for him ... but then he didn't reckon to be doing it himself. In fact, if the men he had hired through a connection of his had done their job right, she was most likely dead already. All he had to do was wait a day or two until they showed up, pay them the other half of what they had been promised, and then hire them to take him out into the desert. If everything went smoothly, the whole thing shouldn't take more than a week or two. Then, he could be hi-tailin' it back to New York.

Still, Adam Tucker was the kind who figured it was best to know your enemy, he'd learned at least that much from his father. Morton, that had been the name he'd been given, when he hired them on. There would still be some time before they'd get back to town and he decided to do a little checking on them on his own.

A few minutes after Adam Tucker had checked into the hotel he came back down the stairs. There was a bounce to his step, and a grim half smile on his lips. To Charlie Harper's way of thinking, this man looked to be one of the coldest he'd run across. He had one of them thin noses that made a man look like he was always testing the wind, like a fox.

'Know anyone in this town by the name of Morton?' Tucker asked sort of uppity like of Charlie as he came up alongside the desk.

Charlie, he nodded. 'There ain't many folks who ain't heard of the Mortons.'

'Well'—Adam was impatient—'where can I find them?'

'Either saloon, or neither saloon,' Charlie

shrugged. 'Them boys get around. Makes it kind of hard for a body to say where they might be.'

Adam stepped out of the hotel on the boardwalk. Charlie gave him the answer he was looking for. The Mortons wouldn't be in town if they were taking care of the job he'd hired them to do, but it wouldn't hurt to see if there might be something he could pick up about them. He stepped off the boardwalk into the street and started for the saloon down the street from Turk's, small puffs of dust rising from beneath his fifty-dollar boots with each step.

The saloon was about what Adam had expected. It was dark. The air was thick with the strangling combination of smoke, dust, alcohol, and sweat. A few months ago, the very thought of going into a place like that would have been enough to almost gag him senseless, but now, he swaggered on inside as if he'd spent half of his life in the roughest bars the West had to offer. Adam's brother had told him a lot about the West. As Western as most men born to it, he had a way of planting pictures in a man's mind of the many things he had seen during the many years he had spent there. Adam had imagined the West, and here it was.

The men sat scattered around the saloon, in little knots. They were at various stages of drunkenness and filth. It wasn't in Adam

55

Tucker to see the dust and sweat on most of the men for what it was. Dirt earned through hard work in a hard land. All his life he'd spent his wits to finding ways of avoiding work of any kind. That some men should actually like their work was something he just couldn't understand.

He walked right up to the bar, but hadn't had a chance to order a drink when a hand tapped him on the shoulder. Adam wheeled around to face a small, black-haired, dark-eyed man with a hard, weathered look about him.

'You look to be the dude we been waiting for,' Abel never had been much for manners or tact. Few good words had been spoken for any of the Mortons when it came to that. 'What's your name, mister?'

'Tucker,' Adam said shortly. 'Adam Tucker, what business is it of yours?'

Abel gestured with his thumb. 'Mr Morton, over there, wants to see you.'

Morton? Adam hadn't expected them to be in town for at least another day. Facing them without knowing a little about them wasn't to his liking, but there was nothing he could do about it right then. He followed the smaller man to a corner table where there were three men. One was black-haired, the other two light, and he took note that the one in the middle sat with his back to the corner. He hardly took time between gulps

56

of food to take notice of Adam's approach. When he finally looked up at Adam, he raised one bushy eyebrow, and looked to be about as friendly as a fisty grizzly.

'I'm Bull Morton,' he growled around a mouthful of food, dropping some crumbs in his wiry black beard. He wiped his shirt sleeve across his mouth and used one ham-sized fist to gesture to the younger men on either side of him. 'These two are my sons. One on my left is Cyrus, the other's Latham. That'n there'—he jabbed a finger toward Abel—'is my nephew, Abel Jenkins.' He let his deep, green eyes meet Adam's. 'Sit down,' he ordered.

The meeting wasn't nothing like Adam had expected, but he'd thought it best to do as the big man said. He pulled up a chair and joined the other three men. The name of Bull fit the big man well. He had broad, meaty shoulders, a thick neck, and a broad tanned face. It was a safe bet the man would touch six foot four when he stood up. His eyes were sharp as an eagle's and his nose was fleshy and flat. Obviously he had been in many fights which hadn't helped his looks none, especially his right ear, which was crumpled like a piece of dried-out leather.

Bull sloshed down half his mug of beer in one gulp, then gave Adam a hard look. 'You the one who hired my son Curley Bill?'

There was no way of telling what Bull

Morton was leading up to, so Adam just nodded silently in answer to his question.

Pushing his empty plate to one side, Bull leaned back in his chair. 'Well, I'll tell you, Tucker, the way this stacks up ... my son is dead, and your niece ain't.' Bull finished his beer and set the empty mug on the table. 'Abel here, he was there when it happened. He told me what happened, and Abel wouldn't lie to me, he's kin. 'Sides, he knows what would happen if I ever found out he lied. The way Abel tells it, Curley Bill, him and a friend, Jed Sloan, took that little girl out in the desert to do what you was paying them for. Abel, he was standing watch at the time. He says that sweet little thing cut down two men with her rifle, and turned him loose in the desert without no gun. Since Bill and Jed were dead, there weren't nothing Abel could do, he come and told me what happened. Bill, he was my youngest, and this whole thing just ain't gonna set right until that girl pays for what she done.' His green eyes were hard and cold when they came to rest on Adam again. 'We're going out tomorrow to make sure she's dead, if'n the Apache ain't done it for us already. The way I see it, it was you got this whole thing rolling, and it'd be right fittin' for you to come along with us.' Bull belched, him never taking his eyes off Adam. 'I'm gonna give you a taste of the desert, boy,' he snapped bitterly. 'My youngest is laying out there dead. He went 'cause 'a you. Reckon we'll be seeing if you have as much sand as him.'

It took a few seconds for what Bull had said to sink in. It just wasn't in him to picture Ann killing two men. There was a whole lot he didn't know about his brother's daughter. Knowing his plan hadn't worked made him feel uneasy, but he wasn't a man to worry about what was done. It was plain to him Bull Morton held him responsible for his son's death, but Adam figured he could take care of himself. He was quick to see if he went with them he'd have the protection of extra guns in Apache territory, and be able to keep an eye out for the landmarks on the map at the same time. With a little luck, when he figured out exactly where the mine was, he could slip away from them and handle things on his own.

Adam nodded. 'I'll be glad to come along,' he said agreeably.

Bull grunted. He was always suspicious of Easterners, no matter what their cut. 'Why do you want her dead anyhow?'

'There's a fortune back East left to her,' Adam said glibly. 'With Ann out of the way, I'd get it all.' The lie slid out easily, without a hitch.

His eyes never leaving Adam, Bull grunted again. A man paying to have one of his own kin murdered was something he didn't take kindly to. It wasn't natural. To a man like Bull, if a man had a bone to pick with kin, he did it himself, not bringing in outsiders and all.

'We're leaving before dawn. You get yourself a outfit and be ready.' Bull Morton got up and left the saloon, his two sons and nephew tagging behind.

Something began tugging at Adam's insides. Was it fear? Was he afraid of the big man? Adam figured himself to be a reasonably brave man, but with Bull Morton one just couldn't be sure. Any man in his right mind would be afraid of a man Morton's size and the power he packed thereabouts, but it bothered Adam. He got up from the table and headed back to the hotel. For a couple of seconds he wondered if maybe he'd bitten off more than he could chew, but then shoved the thought from his mind. It might 'a been better if he'd a taken more time to figure a new course of action, but that gold mine was out there, and he meant to have it.

CHAPTER FIVE

It was a couple hours past sundown when I found the place I was hunting to set up camp. It was a dry wash, deep, and with a cave hollowed out in the bend where the water had rushed by tearing into the sides. The land above the wash was thick with chaparral giving about as much cover as I could hope for. When Ann climbed down off'a her horse she was dead tired and bone weary. I peeled the saddles off them broncs in short order and set up dry camp. There'd be no fire, and that meant eating cold, and no coffee, much as I'd a liked a cup 'bout then. We couldn't risk the fire and we couldn't spare the water. It'd probably be near sunset tomorrow before we come across a waterhole.

As I threw together a camp I noticed Ann was broody and quiet like. She had the grub out putting together a dinner of cold beans and hardtack, but she did a lot of staring out into the desert while she was doing it.

I dragged the saddles and guns up into the back of the shallow cave. Ann followed me inside, handing me some hardtack and beans before she dropped down in the soft sand and began eating her own. It was an odd feeling having a woman beside me on the trail, and it was an unsettling one too. The Apache knew the weaknesses of the white man. He knew that most would rather try to run than expose their women to Apache arrows. Alone, a man had only himself to worry about, and because of that, had a lot better chance of keeping his hair.

Finally breaking the silence that had fallen between us, Ann asked: 'Where did you meet Turk?'

Well, I chuckled as I glanced over at Ann. 'Wondered when you'd get around to askin' that. Turk Billings and me, we go back quite a few years. It's a long story.'

Ann had finished her food and was leaning back against her saddle. 'We have plenty of time.'

She had me there. We sure wasn't going anywhere 'til morning. I took me a little swallow of water to kind of wash down the cold vittles. If I wasn't careful, she'd have me telling her my life story, all the way back to when I'd been a boy in Kentucky.

'I was shanghaied once,' I began. 'I was living in San Francisco, working around the docks some. I was only eighteen at the time. I had this friend, leastways I thought he was a friend. He set me up.' I shook my head, remembering the past and ran a hand through my hair. 'Just shows you what some folks'll do for money.' I looked over at her again. 'You sure you want to hear this?'

Ann nodded, so I went on.

'Well, I wasn't of any mind to stay on ship being as how I hadn't volunteered, so I waited my chance and finally jumped ship off'a New Orleans. Turk, he had himself a bar on the waterfront down in the French quarter. I showed at his place near dawn looking like a river rat gone sour. Old Turk, he was always sort of partial to strays. He took me in and got what happened out of me. Then he hid me out for a few days and got me passage up the river to St Louis. From there, I headed west into the wildest country I could find, and I've been doing it ever since.'

Leaning back, Ann smiled. 'It's hard to believe we come from the same country,' she said, sobering. 'Back East it's parties and civilized talk. Here, it's Apache and bandits.'

'I hadn't thought on it much ma'am.' I picked up Ann's rifle and checked it for a full load. I knew the Apache pretty well, and knowing them meant a man didn't know them at all. It came down to realizing they were men like other men, and like other men, it was hard to figure what they'd be doing next. There were things a body could pick up to help himself, but staying alive depended mostly on keeping your mind free of cobwebs. I checked my own six-gun and rifle, and the gun in Ann's holster. I took the time to punch a couple extra holes in the gunbelt so's it'd fit her better.

Scaring women wasn't something I liked doing, but I figured Ann had better know where she stood. 'You got yourself more trouble'n just Apache,' I told her calmly. 'You left Abel Jenkins alive. He was kin to Curley Bill, and I reckon by now he's found

Bill's pa and told him what happened. You made yourself their personal target when you killed him. Curley Bill's pa has himself a fierce reputation. There ain't much that scares him. I met him once in a poker game in El Paso. He won't let no Apache stand between him and you, so we can figure on him coming after us.'

'Out here?' Ann looked a mite surprised.

Handing back her gun, I shrugged. 'Be more surprised if he don't show, than if he does.'

She glanced over my way, looking some nervous. 'I think I'd better tell you,' she began, 'before he came after me, Bill said something about being paid to get rid of me.'

That shore got my attention. 'Who?'

'I don't know,' Ann answered.

This whole thing was gonna have me walking the fence if something didn't break loose. It was hard to figure how so much trouble could come with one pert little filly like Ann.

'I made it a point not to tell anyone where I was going when I left,' Ann said quickly. Then she frowned, 'Except my uncle. But he wouldn't ... would he?'

'Don't know, it ain't my uncle we're talking about,' I answered.

Ann looked a little sick. 'He would.'

'For the gold.' It wasn't a question, it was a statement. 'Turk said something about your pa finding gold.'

'Yes,' she said softly. 'For the gold. He must have gotten that map from my father. It was never found when he died. Sam had a copy of it, but all I know is what I remember from seeing the map. But I told Uncle Adam when I left that I was going after Jamie.'

'Don't mean much,' I told her. 'Maybe he figures if he was low down enough to steal that map off'a his dead brother, then you might be lying about going after your brother.'

A couple of coyotes called to each other a little ways off. 'You best get out your bedroll and get some rest,' I told her. 'We'll be pulling out 'bout dawn.'

Without saying anything more, Ann turned in, and I leaned back against my saddle to stare up at the desert night. The sky was clear, the moon full, and the stars hung in the dark sky like dew on a spider's web. It reminded me of when I lived up Montana way. I'd had me a wife then. She'd been a lot like Ann. Small and quick. We had us a little spread and little else besides each other, but we knew things would work out. Only been married just shy of a year when that cattle outfit hit town. Pat had been in town picking up some supplies when they got drunk and starting shooting up the town. She took a stray bullet and hung on a whole day, the doctor not being able to do nothing for her. I just sort of drifted since then, not trying to start nothing permanent. Did some sheriffing, but mostly stuck to scouting and some little cowpunching when I got low on cash. A lot of years had passed since then, but a man gets into a way of living, and it's mighty hard to break old habits.

Leaning back against my saddle I closed my eyes. That mustang of mine would warn me if there was someone about, and I was a light sleeper. It looked to me like I'd be catching my sleep in naps for some time to come.

It was coming on to dawn, and I was still dozing when Ann come up on me quiet as an Indian and shook me awake.

'Someone's coming,' she whispered urgently.

Me, I come wide awake like I'd been dumped in a horse trough, and pulled my gun. It wasn't until then that I glanced over at my roan, picketed a short distance away. He was half asleep, taking no notice of anything. A mite short-tempered at having what little sleep I was likely to get interrupted, I sighed and started to tell Anne some night noise must have wakened her.

She shook her head vigorously and stared out into the darkness. 'There's someone coming,' she insisted, 'and there's more than one.'

I was about ready to go into my speech

about the strange noises a body could hear on the desert, that I'd used to reassure other tenderfeet at other times, when that roan brought his head up sharply and stared out into the desert. Nostrils flaring, he tested the still, cool night air, and Ann didn't have to say any more. There was someone coming. It was unnatural, the way she knew before that horse of mine. I didn't figure it possible for anyone to hear something before him, but it looked like I was wrong.

There wasn't time for thinking. We pulled back deeper in the hollow. I had my six-gun out, and Ann had her rifle. Trouble wasn't what we were looking for, but we were ready. It took a few minutes for us to spot them, but when we did we saw three Apache riding along the upper ridge of our dry wash. They moved like phantoms, silent in their passing, and taking no notice of us.

After they'd passed, we stayed quiet a mite longer, just to be on the safe side, then breathed a sigh of relief. They'd come mighty close, and I knew for a fact, it'd happen again. Satisfied they were gone, I slipped my gun back into my holster and stood up. There wasn't no point in trying to catch what little sleep I might get in before dawn, so I broke camp and got ready to move. Trouble was, I couldn't keep from staring at Ann.

'How'd you know about them Indians?' I

asked, real puzzled, when the gear was put together.

'I heard them cutting up the far ridge,' she said softly.

I brushed my hair back and set my worn, dusty hat squarely on my head. Next time that little gal had something to say, I was going to listen up right quick. It never paid a man to go taking chances he didn't have to.

It wasn't too long before sunrise, so we forked our horses and put up some dust heading southeast, deeper into open desert. The country wasn't unfamiliar to me, but coming back wasn't at all like coming home.

CHAPTER SIX

The dawn broke brassy and bright over the desert like it was giving a sample right off of what the rest of the day would be like. Me, I didn't need no advance warning. I'd been through desert country often enough to know what was coming, this day and almost every other day. It'd be three shades hotter than hell by noon, with more of the same saved up for after. There was little difference in the terrain as we pushed slowly south, but what little there was, was for the worse. I was figuring on coming to a rock tank holding water by late afternoon. There had been some heavy rains, this being July. A good many of the hollows made in solid rock by the past centuries of driving rains would be holding water. Some were deep enough to hold it for weeks, some deep enough to hold water for as long as months. The one toward which I was heading was one of the larger ones. I'd used it once when I came through fast, heading north. By now, it should hold plenty of water for us, our horses, and to fill our canteens.

We pushed on slowly, keeping down the dust, and saving the horses. Clumps of ocotillo were scattered around us everywhere. Every time we rested, I made sure it was in amongst a clump of them. It sure beat all how they could give a man cover from unfriendly eyes. I studied the country. It was any man's guess how much farther we'd have to go. From here on out we'd be running across Apache *rancherías* with a mite more regularity. In these parts they didn't bother much to try and hide them camps. There weren't many who'd chance coming this far into their land. And if the Apache weren't enough to keep a man busy, the Mexican Rurales might add a few gray hairs where there weren't none before. I'd never had a run in with them myself, but I'd heard tell they were as apt to shoot a man out of hand as look at him. My being here to stir up the Apache wouldn't be something to put me in their favor.

We come up on a dry stream bed, and I took to following it for a ways on the chance that some of the recent rains might have collected for a time in some of the partially shaded pools along its length. It didn't take me long to figure luck wasn't riding with us, for that stream bed looked as if not a drop of water had trickled down its length in over six months. The only chance left was that pool I knew of higher in the foothills. If that was dry I didn't rightly have a plan for how we'd keep going, but I was sure if it came down to it I'd come up with something. How well a man used his head was what kept him alive in this country.

Touching my horse with my heels, I sent him up the steep east side of the stream bed, heading back up into the hills. Ann never missed a step, she kept right up along behind me, leading the spare horse. When we reached that tank I was counting on, I figured to camp, and rest up good to get an early start the next morning, probably before sunup. Tomorrow, we'd be pushing into the very heart of Apache territory, the Sierra Madres. We were skirting the lower edges of the foothills now. It was in me to wonder how long we'd be able to look for Jamie before the Apache found us. We were walking a tightrope, and bucking a head wind, and I knew it, but we kept right on going. The whole time we were pushing ahead, both of us knew any minute we could be running for all we were worth, high-tailing it for the border, with not even a prayer that we'd make it through.

Glancing back from time to time, I kept an eye on Ann. Her eyes were a-followin' the terrain, and watchin' the same as me. A tenderfoot she might be, but she didn't have no fancy notions about what we were getting into. She rode wary, and a body could almost see her small boots light as a feather in those stirrups, ready to kick free and hit the dirt if danger showed. I'd taken to riding with my rifle out and in my hands a few miles back. I was fixing to stay closer to that rifle than a pretty girl on a cold winter night up in Wyoming.

A little ahead, I spotted me a ridge growing thick with mesquite, and led the way up, figuring to give the horses a breather, and have a look at the surrounding hills before we pushed on. When I looked down off the other side of that ridge through the mesquite, what I saw was enough to have aged me considerable. There, right in the trail that I'd been following, was a war party of six Apache. I eased that roan of mine to a stop. The urge to pull up short was strong in me, but I knew a sharp motion would draw their attention. I warned Ann to silence, but I needn't have worried none for there was

71

something holding their attention that I
hadn't seen when I first looked that way.
Them Apache had themselves a prisoner. It
was like a little clearing below. It was a
hollow between a couple of small hills, but
the bottom was flat and sandy, and the side
of one hill was thick with mesquite while the
other had only a few clumps of ocotillo. The
ridge from where I was watching formed,
more or less, the third side of a rounded
triangle around the hollow, though it was
higher than either of the other two hills. Ann
come up beside me, quiet like, and glanced
down where I was looking while I dug out a
pair of Army field glasses to get me a better
look. Below, I could make out them six
'Pache like they weren't more than two feet
away. I could see their broad, flat faces, their
brown bodies lean as hungry wolves. But I
was looking past them to their prisoner. I'd
say he was in his early twenties. His skin was
lighter than that of most desert riders I'd
seen, but his hair was coal black, and his
dark eyes seemed to be staring through that
mesquite right at me. They had him staked
out in the sand, spread-eagled and stripped
to the waist. A small fire burned close beside
his head, and through the glasses I could see
the red hot glow of the coals. Them Indians
had already worked over his chest and left
arm pretty good. From what I knew about
Apache, and if I was any judge, their party

was just getting started. The captive had himself a wicked-looking gash low down on his right side. Probably picked that up when the Indians cornered him. From the general look of things, he'd fought like a she bear protecting her young. I lowered the field glasses and slipped them back into my saddlebags, giving thought to the situation. It wasn't in me to just ride off and leave him to the Apache, but I knew that whatever I decided to do, I'd have to do mighty quick. Them Indians figured they had all the time in the world, and they were going at it slow, but it wouldn't be too long 'til that boy was too weak to make his break, even if I gave him his chance. And one thing was for sure. I couldn't risk coddling anybody while Ann was with me. When I got that boy loose, he was on his own. Maybe all I would do was buy him a quick death, but the way I saw it, even that was better than what the Indians had in mind for him. Pondering a few more seconds, I turned my horse down the trail.

'You're not going to leave him?' Ann mouthed the words softly.

I shook my head and pulled up close to her. 'No,' I spoke in a whisper, conscious of every sound we made. 'I was figuring on giving him a hand if I could. Trouble is,' I added, 'I can't do that without some shooting, and that means every Apache in these mountains will know we're here. That,'

I pointed out, 'is going to make it that much harder to find your brother without losing our own scalps.'

'We'll get back all right, and with Jamie,' Ann said with a firm confidence I wasn't up to right then.

I shrugged and pointed her in the right direction. 'Just keep heading south and try to keep out of sight ... I'll catch up.'

Ann didn't argue. She nodded silently and moved off, leading our spare horse. I watched her go, cautiously skirting the area close to the Indian camp, then picking up speed as she got clear of the area. I had to give her credit for using her head. She hadn't made a careless or stupid move on the trail since we'd joined up together a couple days back. Four days out from Tucson and here I was hunting Injun trouble.

When I was sure Ann was clear, I moved off along the ridge, riding bent low in the saddle to keep from brushing the canopy of mesquite that had sprung up around me. I eased my way off the back side of the ridge a little ways down, figuring to slip up between the two hills and lay my hands on them Indians' ponies. They were all tied in a tight little knot on the lower fringes of the mesquite on the far hill. It should be real easy for me to get close and stir things up a bit. Working my way up close as I dared, I brought my rifle up. How this was going to work out wasn't clear to me, but I had me a full load in that rifle and by the time it was emptied I figured something would show itself.

Taking careful aim, I squeezed off the first shot. The bullet hit the stake that held the prisoner's right hand square. He didn't waste no time trying to figure what happened. He just gave that wrist a couple of good tugs and the rope split, freeing one hand while I dropped the Apache closest to him with my second shot. That Indian just folded up across the fire, dead, and their black-haired captive, not one to miss a chance, grabbed for the knife the dead Indian was carrying. He got himself a hold on that knife about the time I dropped another one of the Indians that was trying to throw down on him from the edge of the sandy clearing. I kept the lead flying, keeping them Indians pinned down behind some rocks while their prisoner hacked his way through them ropes and ducked for some cover his ownself. Well, that was all I'd been waiting for. I scrambled back to that roan of mine, and hit the saddle leather. I swung him hard around, heading for them Indian ponies. Grabbing the dangling reins of a pony that looked to have a lot of run in him I scattered the rest with a wild yell and a couple of shots. I come fogging it down between those two little hills, leading that cream and brown paint and

cutting loose with a few more shots just to let
them Apache know I wasn't forgetting them.
Them Indians weren't forgetting me neither.
They had rifles, and they were using them.
Bullets were kicking up dust around the feet
of my horse and whipping past my ears. I'd
ducked more'n my share of lead, but that
didn't keep a man from getting nervous
every time it happened, for I'd picked up a
few in my time as well. Them slugs were
hitting mighty close, and me all the time
knowing I couldn't take a slug and be any
good out here. Me, I was sweating, more out
of fear for Ann if I got myself shot up, than
for myself. That young fella seen me come
around the base of that hill, and he didn't
need no explaining to know what was
expected. He come out of those rocks where
he'd been sprawled for cover and vaulted up
on that pony's bare back like it was the most
natural thing in the world. Those injuries
weren't slowing him down neither when he
pulled that pony sharp around and we lit out
of there, lead whistling all around us, like the
devil was on our tails. A couple good, long
strides took us out of range behind a hill, and
there just wasn't anything but luck to explain
how we managed to get clear with our skins
whole.

That little paint was a game horse, keeping
right up there with my roan at a dead out
run. Neither one of us was thinking of

anything except putting a lot of country between them Indians and us. Trouble was, this was their country. Now, they'd be riding wary, keeping an eye peeled for strangers. We rode together for a piece, that dark-haired fellow and me, and every once in a while I could see him looking my way, them deep-set black eyes of his sharp, like they was sizing me up. He was a'trying to yell something to me, but the wind snatched most of the words away leaving only a mess of mixed-up words hanging on the wind. There wasn't no time for talk, only traveling. After a while he started pointing off to the west and waving like I should go with him. Shaking my head, I pointed south. A deep furrow crossed his smooth forehead as he frowned and looked at me like I was plumb loco. I couldn't blame him, that same thought had crossed my mind a time or two the last few days. He tried again, but I still shook my head. Finally he just grinned, shrugged, and pointed that pony's nose west. He had him a place in mind, there wasn't no doubt of that, probably a place to hole up and maybe get some help, if I was any judge. Alone, I'd light a shuck with him, but right now, I had me a little gal that needed catching up with ... and right quick.

I pushed my roan hard, cutting deeper south and working my way into the hills. I was just getting around to worrying about

Ann when I spotted her working her way down a rocky hillside, still leading our spare horse. Relaxing some, I looked to see where she'd come from. There was a heavy growth of brush and some rock further up the side of the hill. It didn't look like much, but she'd stayed quiet amongst it, and would have gone unnoticed even by me if she hadn't started down. That girl had natural trail savvy, even if she didn't show too much good sense in traipsing out here in the first place. She eased that horse of hers down off the hill, eying my lathered-up mount.

She looked at me all round-eyed and expectant. 'What happened?'

Well, I give it to her short and simple, not bothering with no details. 'He lit out almost due west,' I added when I'd finished. 'That young fella was covering ground faster'n a high rolling desert jack rabbit, and showing a helluva lot more sense than some folks I could mention,' I finished pointedly.

Laughing softly, Ann swung in behind me. That girl had her mind set, and there wasn't any changing it.

We pushed on a ways, going some slower so as not to push my roan. When I figured we were as clear of that trouble I stirred up with those Apache as we were likely to get, I switched horses to give my own a breather. That desert bred roan of mine didn't like it one bit when I climbed into the saddle of that big boned, sandy colored horse that had belonged to Curley Bill. He'd been doing nothing but coming along at the end of a lead line for a couple of days now, and he was ready to go. That roan of mine didn't like the idea of being led. He snorted and stamped some, but didn't give us any real trouble. The little steeldust Ann rode never seemed to get tired. He carried his much lighter burden with ease and climbed the hill trails like he was second cousin to a mountain goat. A man always had his eye out for good horseflesh, and the way that steeldust moved, he looked to be one of the best.

It was coming on to early evening when we reached that rock tank I'd been figurin' on. It was filled plumb up to the brim with good water. I threw together a camp, unsaddled our horses and then gave that roan of mine some extra attention. In this country it was a good idea for a man to be friends with his horse. Many a man crossing the desert found out his horse was the only friend he had.

When the darkness settled in I took the first watch. I knew what was coming. We were right in the thick of Apache land, but it was gonna take some doing to find Jamie out here. The *rancherías* would be spread out. All we could do was try and check each one we come on. There just plain wasn't any other way. Them Indians might 'a been pretty

79

scattered out, but the problem came when they used talking smoke to let their brothers up the trail know somebody was a'comin'. Looked to me like we were gonna get ourselves worked in pretty tight. From now on, what we'd been through would seem like a picnic in the woods. Tomorrow, we'd start the real climbing. Up off the desert floor, we'd probably get into some pines, and oaks, but we'd also be right at the back door of the Apache. If I remembered rightly, we should come across one of their *rancherías* pretty quick. Apache move around quite a bit, and even though their camp may be in the same area, it doesn't mean it'll be in the same spot. And once we reached the camp, there was the problem of trying to locate the boy. Once we did that, it was anybody's guess what would come next.

The cool darkness was like a tonic to me, for I am a man who likes the wild country more than anything else. I glanced around our small camp. How many other times had I stood watch in camps just like this one? Too many to remember, that was for danged sure. But I had other things to remember. It was hard for a body to realize how long ago it was that I was a boy back in the Kentucky hills. Even then, I'd found the wildest, high-up places I could. Of course, my pa'd been with me then. He taught me all I knew about the woods, hunting, and shooting and such. It had been a real good life 'til ma died and pa took it into his head to lite out for California. We'd ended up in San Francisco, not a good place for a boy with a hankering for the wide open spaces. Pa, he finally died of some cough he'd picked up and I was about to head on out on my own when that ex-friend of mine got me shanghaied.

The horses were standing quiet. For the moment, there was nothing out there to draw their attention. Ann was sleeping. I sat with legs crossed, my rifle across my knees, gazing out across the open, rolling desert. It seemed alive in the faint glow of the quarter moon, like a quiet sea at peace. Now it was calm, but the desert, like the sea, can hide its violent savagery underneath a surface that is real quiet 'til the full force of the storm is pounding on you. I picked me up another piece of jerky and commenced to chewing on it. There were still long hours before I would wake Ann to stand watch while I caught a couple hours of sleep.

CHAPTER SEVEN

If nothing else, Adam Tucker had to admit to a grudging respect for Bull Morton. When they'd rode out of Tucson just before dawn, people had peeked cautiously from their windows, and men on the street had turned to watch their passing. Nobody seemed to cross Bull Morton. It made Adam sit a little taller in the saddle knowing all them were afraid of Bull Morton, and he, Adam Tucker, was riding with him. It was exhilarating to feel as though you held the power of life and death right in the palm of your hand so that men looked your way with a mixture of fear, awe, and respect. Power is a heady wine that packs a powerful kick. It gave a man pause to have another look at the world. The only thing that could outweigh the light-headed feeling of power was the money Adam was planning to get out of that mine. The Mortons were strong, but they weren't rich. The power wealth gave a man was something Adam respected above else.

The first day, Abel Jenkins had led them out to the spot where he said Ann had killed Curley Bill and Jed Sloan with a rifle. Adam, he still found it hard to believe that Ann had somehow managed to gun down two professional gunmen. It didn't make sense to him that the frail little girl he remembered could have shot down two men. Still, any cornered animal would fight, and all of Adam's doubts couldn't change the cold fact of the two graves left inside the remains of what had been a camp.

The graves had been a surprise to everyone, including Abel Jenkins. They'd been figuring on finding two bodies.

'You do this?' Bull snapped at Abel.

Abel shook his head. 'I told ya' Bull,' he whined, 'I didn't have time to do nothing.'

'Then who the hell else is out here gallavantin' around? The girl couldn't have had the strength to dig in this hard ground,' Bull growled as he stepped down from a horse that was big enough to carry two men Abel's size all day without hardly raising a sweat.

Abel gave his uncle a look resembling a whipped pup and shrugged. 'Beats me, Bull.'

Bull turned on Abel like a wildcat. 'Then pile down out of that saddle pronto, and fix them beady eyes of your'n in the dirt.' He exploded. 'You ain't been a helluva lot of help to me lately, boy.' Bull cursed him freely and thoroughly, throwing an angry look in the direction of his two remaining sons.

Cyrus had already been climbing down from his horse when his pa exploded. It was nothing new to him. That same fury had been directed at him a time or two. Cyrus, he was twenty-four, younger than his brother Latham, and about a year older than Curley Bill had been. It added some to our problems that he was a natural born tracker. He'd been following trails of one sort or another since the time he was knee-high to a hound pup. He wiped the sweat from his broad, sun-browned forehead with a dusty sleeve and resettled his hat on his thick crop of sandy brown hair. A thick handlebar mustache of a little darker color drooped above his upper lip. Cyrus was lacking in the enormous build of his pa, but he did resemble him a mite in the features. There was a grim, hardened look about them flinty gray eyes of his, framed by heavy brown eyebrows. A vicious looking scar ran the length of the right side of his face, which didn't add none to his looks. By making some pretty dumb mistakes as a youngun he had learned the ways of the world. One of the first things he learned was that it was almost certain suicide not to have the face to go along with being a Morton. Curley Bill had never had the face. It had been soft, and now he was dead. The soft look of Curley Bill may not have been the whole reason for him getting himself killed, but it was a good marker to go by. Cyrus'd counted himself lucky when he picked up that scar. Only his pa and brothers knew he'd gotten it when he'd been working on a pump out behind their place, and a piece of metal broke off, flying up into his face. It had laid his face open to the bone. Cyrus was a mighty peculiar Morton, him never liking to fight. Even so, folks'd found out he could handle himself all right if need be, his pa'd seen to that. That scar had kept him from having to prove up more times than he liked to think about. There was something about a mean-looking scar, and the name of Morton, that made folks kind of naturally want to walk wide around a man.

Glancing over toward his brother, Cyrus could see Latham was already with their pa, Bull, giving his thoughts on the situation. There was no doubts in his mind, Latham had always been Bull's favorite. He was the oldest, and aside from Bull, he was the strongest. Latham even looked more like Bull than either Curley Bill or Cyrus. He had the same fleshy, oversized nose, and the same general build, though not quite as big, and the same green eyes. There was something about those eyes though that Cyrus had never liked, and a lot of other folks felt the same way. Folks who'd managed to run crossways of him. There was a coldness about them that made Cyrus a mite nervous at times. There was no mistaking he was Bull Morton's son. Even in those things that Latham was different, he was still the same. His hair was light brown instead of black like Bull's, and his squared off jaw was clean shaven, but he was a Morton through and through. His skin was burned almost black by the desert sun, and lined deeply. Latham sure didn't need a beard like Bull, or a mustache like his brother to have that hard, unbending look about him. When Latham walked, it was with the same self-assurance, the same arrogance that Bull had. It was a family trait lacking in Cyrus.

There were tracks a plenty at his feet when Cyrus started having himself a look around. More tracks than could be made by a camp of four people were scattered everywhere a body looked. Cyrus knew what they meant.

'Apache been here, Pa,' Cyrus told his father with a mite of reluctance. Somehow, he always felt as if he was breaking into something when Latham and Bull were together.

Bull nodded impatiently. 'So many damn pony tracks, it ain't possible to find nothing else.'

Cyrus just kept on looking. It was near always possible to find something if a body just kept a'lookin'. Indian ponies weren't shod, and the ones they were looking for were. A partial track, a scarred stone, anything to give him a direction was all Cyrus needed. He wasn't sure he knew exactly what was going on, it never seemed that he did. It was real hard for Cyrus to believe Curley Bill would try to kill a woman, but then most things Curley Bill had done in the past were hard for him to believe. He'd never tried to figure the actions of his younger brother. Curley Bill had been family, and family was the only loyalty that

Cyrus knew.

It took a little time, but Cyrus finally found what he was looking for. Near a clump of prickly pear was a rock that spelled out real clear that it was scarred by the recent passing of a shod hoof.

'Think I've got something,' Cyrus called the others over to have a look at his find.

Bull grunted his satisfaction. 'You reckon them Apache took them off?' he asked his son.

Cyrus shook his head. 'From the looks of this I'd say they left different times. Don't even look like them Indians was interested in following.'

Bull cursed loud and long. There was a feeling about him that gave a body a feeling that here was a man looking for a likely face to plant his fist in. 'We'll have to keep going then,' he snapped. 'Ain't nothing ever gets done the easy way for us.' Spinning on his heel, Bull stomped back to his horse.

Cyrus was figuring this would be a sure enough tricky business, so he hung back some as Latham strode along beside Bull. Tracking would not be easy, and they were already trespassing on Apache land. It was a risk in this land every time a man set foot out a door. Pushing their luck was something Cyrus didn't take kindly to.

As they pulled out, Adam Tucker rode up alongside Cyrus. Cyrus didn't hold any good feelings for the man, although he couldn't have said for sure just what it was about the Easterner that made him get a prickly feeling up his spine. He'd been surrounded by brutality all his life, but with Bull, family always came first. It stuck in Cyrus's craw that this Adam Tucker wanted his own niece dead. Killing a woman didn't set right with Cyrus, and if it came down to it, he didn't rightly know what was in his mind to do about it.

'Thought I'd be seeing wild red Indians coming over every hill,' Adam Tucker said to Cyrus with a chuckle. 'Certainly seems quiet enough to me.'

Cyrus glanced sideways at Adam. Letting his gray eyes look the man over real cool like. 'Be surprised what can happen out here, Mr Tucker,' he said flatly. 'Apache are notional. There's no telling what's on their minds 'til they reckon it's time to do something.'

Shrugging, Adam laughed. 'You sure you people out here aren't exaggerating just a little to keep us Easterners guessing as to exactly what's going on out here?'

'You keep thinking thataway, mister,' Cyrus said sharply, 'and it won't be long 'til you're roastin', head down, over an Apache fire.'

Realizing he'd made a mistake in saying what he had to Cyrus, Adam real sensibly left things as they were, and rode on into the desert with nothing more to say. It wouldn't pay to make an enemy of the Mortons ... just yet.

Camp was set up before full dark, Cyrus picking the site with plenty of mesquite to break up the smoke from a fire Bull was sure to demand. He knew his pa to be a reckless man, and it wouldn't pay a body to try to change his mind on anything. Trouble was, this time, Cyrus reckoned it was more than himself Bull was risking. And it always made Cyrus some edgy when Latham stood by Pa in his way of thinking, no matter what. Abel was a different story. He'd been raised with the family, but the man was a weasel. Since they were kids, Cyrus had known that about Abel. He was always around to start trouble going, but never around to finish it. That part had always been left up to Latham, Cyrus, and Curley Bill. Cyrus took to the camp chores as soon as they found a spot. Latham and Bull were over by some rocks having themselves a parley, and Abel, as usual, was standing right close by. The only one Cyrus couldn't spot was that dude they were dragging across the desert, Adam Tucker. Cyrus frowned, then shrugged. What the hell, it was Tucker's skin if he wanted to be wandering around out there somewhere.

Adam had slipped off from camp. He was sure none of the others had noticed him. He

89

wasn't one to be foolhardy so he hadn't gone far, just far enough for some privacy. Up to now, he hadn't made up his own mind yet whether the danger from the Indians was real or merely a good yarn, but it wouldn't pay to be reckless when so close to his goal. When he knew for sure no one was looking, he took the leather pouch from around his neck and opened it flat. As far as he could tell, they were moving in the right direction, heading for the gold mine. As they had been riding, he had recognized a few of the landmarks leading up to the mine. Jack had been an excellent map maker. A youngster could have followed the map his brother had drawn. He eagerly searched the piece of leather he held in his hands for the next landmark that would place him even closer to his dead brother's mine.

It was just about then that Bull glanced up from where he'd been talking with his oldest son, and looked around the camp. Cyrus was there on the far side of the camp, working as usual, but that Tucker fella was nowhere in sight.

'Damn fool idjut tinhorn,' Bull snapped. It didn't turn a hair with him whether Adam managed to get himself killed or not. What did rile him was the thinking that if the Apache found him wandering around, they'd just naturally start to looking for others. Bull did as he pleased, but he figured that everybody else had better do as he wanted.

Lunging to his feet, Bull stomped off in the only direction Adam could have taken to get out of camp without anyone taking notice. With only the dim light of the quarter moon to guide him, Bull picked his way amongst the cactus and rocks, working his way to where he figured to find Adam. Latham and Abel knew better than to follow Bull when he went storming off thataway. A long time ago, they had learned that it wasn't advisable to go tagging along unless they had a special invite.

There wasn't a whole lot of ground for Bull to cover before he spotted Adam standing inside the shielding front of mesquite, his back turned and head bowed as if he was staring intently at something. Now Bull was a curious man, and it seemed a mite strange to him that this Easterner, fresh off the stage, would be likely to go wandering around the desert alone without a real good reason. There was always a reason for everything, and Bull figured to find out what Adam's was. On cat feet, with a silence that seemed nigh impossible for a man of his bulk, Bull crept forward.

'What've you got there?' Bull demanded sharply.

Adam spun around to face Bull, at the same time fumbling to hide the map, but Bull's hand shot out with the speed of a

91

striking snake and grabbed the piece of leather from Adam's hands. Bull's sharp green eyes went from Adam to the map in his hands and back again. He frowned, deep furrows appearing in his broad forehead, and he set to scratching his chin real thoughtful like through his wiry black beard.

For certain, the piece of leather couldn't be mistaken for anything else but a map. Bull grinned broadly. 'You been holding out on us, Tucker?' His voice was quiet, like the low growling of a threatening wolf.

Adam returned Bull's smile, but it was a mite thin. 'It's not important,' he said trying to weasel out of the situation. 'It's only something from my brother. It's all I have to remember him by.'

There was a silence that must have seemed to Adam to last forever, then Bull, he about busted his buttons laughing. 'You expect me to swallow that? You bein' the same fella who came all the way out here to find your niece so's you kin kill her?' The laughter died down, then Bull turned menacingly toward Adam. 'Now suppose you tell me what it really is you got there, and no more of them fancy lies of yourn.'

He'd made a lot of mistakes in his time, but Adam wasn't a fool. He hadn't been careful enough and now he'd been caught. There was no way he could lie his way out of it. He would only be kidding himself if he thought he could stay with the Mortons now and still manage to slip off to see about that there gold mine with Bull knowing about the map.

Adam sighed. 'It's a map to a gold mine. That's the fortune my brother left to his family. And the way it looks to me, that's where we'll find Ann.'

'Well, I'll be...' A deep chuckle rolled up from the hollow of Bull's belly. That ol' gold fever was creeping up on Bull mighty fast.

'There's plenty there.' Adam was acting kind of timid. 'We could split fifty-fifty.'

'I was thinking more like sixty-forty,' Bull stated flatly. 'I got me two boys and a nephew to support.'

Licking his lips nervously, Adam nodded. He was cornered. There wasn't a whole lot he could do but agree, not unless he wanted to take on all four of the Mortons now. But there might be a chance later. If he bided his time, there might still be a chance of getting the entire mine for himself. He'd have to wait and watch. Things have a way of working themselves out, if they have a little help ... and he figured himself to be the man who could do the helping.

Bull strode back to camp carrying the map in one beefy hand. 'We got us some good news, boys. Mr Tucker, here, has decided to share his gold mine with us, and we ain't too far from it right now. That's where we're

93

heading, come morning.'

'What about that girl, Pa?' Latham asked real angry like. 'The one what shot Curley Bill and Jed?'

'Tucker, here, says that's where his niece is likely to be. If she ain't, there'll be plenty of time to go looking for her later.' Bull thundered, 'You only get a crack at a gold mine once in a lifetime, boys. Curley Bill would understand that.' In that much Bull was right. Curley Bill would have put a gold mine over revenge any day.

Latham looked away in disgust, but knew better than to say anything once Bull had made a decision. Cyrus glanced at Adam, contempt flashing from his eyes, then went back to work. It didn't matter all that much to Cyrus what they did. It didn't seem to him Bull was interested in asking what he thought anyway. Besides, it wasn't in him to believe there really was a gold mine, leastways not 'til he saw it with his own eyes.

CHAPTER EIGHT

I was laying belly down in a sandy hollow I'd worked out for myself on the top of a hill overlooking the Apache *ranchería*. It was getting on to noon, and it was hot. The hot desert sand was burning through my shirt,

94

and my eyes were stinging with the sweat that was running into them, but still I kept combing that camp below me with them old Army field glasses of mine hoping to catch sight of a youngster that could be Ann's brother.

We'd been riding a streak of luck, longer than I cared to remember for fear of it coming to an inconvenient end. The hollow where I lay was screened by a thick growth of stunted, twisted pines fringing the hill where it dropped off into the valley below. We'd climbed to maybe five thousand feet. There was still plenty of mesquite around, and here and there a sparse patch of grass. But the only thing to hold my interest was the Apache camp below. We'd been there up on that hill crest too long for safety already, but I'd caught a glimpse of a white boy in the camp, and I lingered, always hoping for one more look. Ann was up behind me tending to keeping the horses quiet, and I'd said nothing about the boy to her, not wanting to get her hopes too high.

The only thing we had working for us was those Apache figuring there wasn't anyone loco enough to come riding right up to their camp. Some guards were posted, but they weren't rightly paying attention to what they were supposed to be doing. It was natural enough. I hadn't heard of anyone else loco enough to come this far into their stronghold. Leastways, if they had, they hadn't gotten out again to let the world know about it.

My eyes squinted up against the eyepieces of those field glasses as I took me a deep breath and kept waiting. Squaws were always working, busy with one thing or another. There were some children playing around the camp, but since I'd had one quick look at the white youngster disappear into a wickiup, I'd seen no more of him. My nerves were strung out tight as a bow string, and my patience was wearing thin.

The sound of galloping hoofs reached my ears, and a hunting party of four braves rode into camp, the dust swirling up around them. Seemed like most of the camp came out to meet them. It was plain to see the braves had had themselves a good day, and the meat passed down to the waiting hands was a sure enough welcome sight to the rest of the camp. That boy come out of the wickiup too. He stood off a little from the Indians, and I'll be danged if he didn't look to be staring right in my direction. It was right then I got me a good look at that boy. He was white, there was no question about that. His light brown hair was long and shaggy, hanging nearly to his eyes. He looked a mite tall for eleven, but I reckon boys that age grow quickly. Those glasses I was using brought him so close I thought I could count the freckles on his upturned nose. Either that boy down there was Jamie Tucker or as close to a twin as he was likely to get. The picture of him that Ann had shown me had been of a younger boy in years and experience, but there was no mistaking him.

That lucky streak we'd been riding was holding. This was only the second camp I'd bellied up close enough to to have me a good look-see around. I'd found the boy, but there was still the problem of how to get him out. The Apache must have figured he'd have nowhere to run for he wasn't closely watched. A boy on foot wouldn't have had a chance getting clear of those hills, let alone take on the desert that surrounded them. With Ann and me to back him up his chances didn't look to be a whole lot better, but we'd come this far, and there was no turning back.

Slowly, I worked my way back to where I'd left Ann with the horses and told her what I'd found while I packed my field glasses back into my saddlebags. It didn't seem a big surprise to her that he was there, and she was eager to get on with the job of getting him out. It hadn't been Ann's but my idea, to stop at that first camp and look it over. There, she'd been skittish, and of a mind to push on, heading in this direction like a bloodhound hot on a trail.

Well, it wasn't much of a plan that I had,

in fact there wasn't a plan at all. But, there wasn't a whole lot that could be planned in a situation like this. A man had to bide his time and do what had to be done when trouble showed. About all I could do was to leave Ann alone with the horses while I worked my way down there and came back with Jamie. That last part about coming back with Jamie was a hope in me that the lucky streak we'd been riding didn't break, and the Apache didn't slow us down.

Out of old habit, I checked my handgun for a full load, then slipped off into the brush and started working my way down the steep hillside. There was plenty of scrub brush to hide me as I moved, careful like, down the slope. Sounds from the Apache camp drifted up to me as I drew closer. Ponies snorted. A short distance away, with her back turned to me, was a squaw pounding some grain into flour, and a little past her the Apache hunters spoke in loud voices of the hunt. I could see the smoke of the cook fires, and the faint smell of venison drifted past my nose.

No one spotted me, but I was nervous as a cat when I reached the bottom of the hill. It seemed as if prickly pear and cholla were always underfoot as I skirted the edge of the Indian camp, making my way around to where I'd last seen that boy. Ocotillo spread out all over that sunken valley like fans, and the strange part of it was the distant hills harbored oaks and pines and even some thick grasses as a man reached the higher slopes. The boy was moving off toward the wickiup when I come up from behind. If he went inside again, I'd have me a hatful of trouble. I took me a couple of long strides and hunkered down behind the wickiup where I could see, real good, at least part of the camp.

Jamie was coming across the camp, but instead of heading for the wickiup opening, he come on past, like he was looking for something. Most likely gathering firewood for the cook fires. This wasn't no time to stand on ceremony. When he came around the side of that wickiup, I reached out and grabbed him, slapping one gritty hand over his mouth.

For a few seconds there, I thought I'd laid a hold of a wildcat. That was one kid with a lot of fight.

'You want to get back to your sister?' I whispered urgently as I held his squirming body fast to the ground.

Well, that was all it took. He settled down right quick and turned half around to get a better look at me. He stared at me through brown eyes, large around like his sister's. 'Ann?' he asked in a whisper to match my own.

I nodded and let him get up. 'She's up in them hills holding the horses,' I told him.

'We best rattle our hocks out of here. Them Indians are liable to take themselves a notion to start looking for you.'

Up that hillside together we went, me a mite in the lead, but Jamie following along behind as close as a body could. I could scarce hear him coming so I glanced back from time to time, kind of keeping an eye out for him. It was something I needn't have bothered to do though, that kid was wearing Apache moccasins, and moved like a Indian himself. He'd learned a lot during his three months with the Indians. And he was dressed like an Apache, wearing breechcloth, tunic, headband, and high moccasins.

Just as fast as we could get one foot in front of the other, we climbed that hill keeping to the brush for cover. Seconds dragged by, and the muscles along my spine were tight, waiting for the first cry of alarm to come from below. If we got pinned on that slope, it could sure enough end right there.

Somehow we made it up to the crest where Ann was waiting with the horses. When she caught sight of Jamie coming right up behind me, her eyes lit up and a smile that looked like the first rays of dawn spread across her face. Jamie ran over to his sister and threw himself into her arms.

'There's no time!' I whispered hoarsely, and more sharply than I should have. Thing was, all I could think of was them Apache breathing down our necks. We needed every second we could get.

Having more sense than to take offense, Ann nodded shortly and moved away from her brother. She stepped into her steeldust's saddle, and Jamie vaulted into the saddle of that sandy colored horse that had been Curley Bill's. I reined my roan around and took the lead. Ann fell in second, and Jamie brought up the rear. When I looked at that boy, I could see there was a lot of man in him. It would likely be a shock to Ann to find out just how much he'd changed, providing we got clear of this place with our skins whole.

I led the way off the crest of them hills, and onto the slopes right quick, knowing how easy it was to spot a body when he was skylining himself. The Apache knew the same thing, and they'd be looking for it. We picked our way between the rocks and cactus, and skirted a couple of dwarfed and twisted pines that clung with fierce determination to the crest of the hill, their roots more out of the ground than in.

There was a stillness inside of me. Thinking, trying to figure the best direction, trying to gauge how much the horses had to give, and trying to remember where there was water. I had years of experience to draw on, and before this was over, I'd need every bit of it. The Apache would know of our need for water. No living thing could go without it for long, at least none that I'd found, and the Apache's first move would be to set out to cover the waterholes. Just because we had a lead on them didn't mean they couldn't catch up and pass us. This was their country, they knew the side trails, and I had only my instinct and certain signs for direction to depend on. I had been across this country but once before, alone, and it had been a close thing. Mostly, I knew only those things that I'd been told about the desert that spread out at the foot of the mountains. There were no guarantees, but there were some places where water most likely would be found. I could feel the dust and grit on my face, and the sweat in my hair beneath my hat. We urged our horses forward, pushing them. For the moment, I wanted nothing more than to get clear of those hills before all hell broke loose, and there was nowhere to run. We were far enough now from the Indian camp, so's we wouldn't be able to hear when the alarm was raised. From here on out, it would be only guesswork and pure luck to get us through.

Moving fast, and giving our horses only short rests until well after dark, we pushed on. After dark, I didn't feel any safer, but our horses had to have a good breather or they'd fold. I spotted a large hollow just below the trail we'd been following, and pulled up there, hoping the mesquite that grew in clumps around us would be enough to shield the three of us from prying eyes should the Apache get too close before we saw or heard them. Ann passed out a cold meal of jerky and biscuits while I stood watch. With a little luck, it shouldn't be much past dawn when we got out of these hills and onto the open desert. It was exchanging one hell for another, but always we were getting that much closer to safety. I smiled grimly at my own faith that we'd reach a settlement or fort before them Apache ran us down. The way I figured it, there just wasn't any way, leastways none that I could see, for us to get through without a fight. We were still a mite better than four days out of Tucson.

I glanced over at Ann and Jamie. They'd stretched out on the ground to catch a couple hours sleep. Next stop we made I'd have to do the same or I'd be hanging by a mighty fine string before too long. The horses stood quiet. There wasn't so much as a coyote close by to stir them up. The night sky was clear, and the stars hung down close to the earth like a bunch of fireflies. There was a cool, soft touch to the air surrounding me, and a gentle breeze coming through the hills. It was easy to see how a man could fall in love with wild country like this. Years ago the country hereabouts got under my skin, and it wasn't likely I'd ever rid myself of the feeling. There were times of peace, such as now, even when danger was all around, that a man couldn't find anywhere else. I hunkered down on one knee just outside our camp, and let my eyes pass slowly over the countryside. Nothing stirred. It wasn't that I expected anything to show, yet, but it didn't pay a man to underestimate the Apache.

It was just before dawn when we pulled up stakes, me not having seen any Indians while we were holed up resting. Our horses were a lot fresher after the rest, and we picked our way down the last of the steep slopes as the sun was lighting up the east sky. The country was rough and wild, but the going would be some easier now that we were clear of the high mountains.

The country was more rolling now, but off in the distance I could see the rugged peaks of some short, scattered sawtooth ranges, jabbing their peaks into the sky. Seemed to me, as we rode amongst the forest of cactus that surrounded us, that most everything that grew in the desert came with thorns. We were riding easy, saving our horses and keeping the dust down when I glanced up our sidetrail, and caught sight of sunlight flashing on a rifle barrel. It was kind of dim and hard to see, but I'd seen that flash too often not to recognize it.

Pulling my roan up short, I let out a yell as

the first shot split the air and kicked up dirt in front of my horse's feet. The second shot came some closer, whistling past my ear as I wheeled my horse around, pointing his nose toward the northwest, and Ann and Jamie followed my lead. We leaped those horses into a run as the Indians came spilling over the rocks and amongst the greasewood, firing as they tried to close in their ambush. Another band of Apache showed themselves right in front of us. We cut our running horses hard to the left, swinging around as they took out after us, then swung back almost due north as we skirted a low hill.

Them Indians were strung out behind us, and coming on fast when Ann started signaling for us to turn due west. Now I knew that if we turned that way we'd be brushing up mighty close to them Indians tailing us, and each stride we took would put us that much farther from Tucson. Trouble was, we just weren't going to make it this way, and I wasn't in no position to argue with a body who had a suggestion.

Well, we peeled off to the west, and the Apache moved to cross our trail. But we had three mighty fine horses under us, and they stretched out low on the run like they knew it was up to them to pull us out of this one. For the moment, the ground was hard, the strides of the horses jarring, but fast. Glancing over my shoulder back toward the north I saw that third Apache war party appear, boiling over the ridge of a dry wash that had been invisible to us. It was plain, the other two bunches had been to herd us into the third. We'd have run headlong into them if we hadn't changed directions. I was holding my roan down, staying a little behind, and to one side of Ann and Jamie's running mounts. If we didn't find some way to give our horses a rest, we were going to run them to death, and the Apache would be down on us like a swarm of locust.

Then I saw it. A dry wash splitting the desert open before us, and off to the south a cluster of low hills. It wasn't much of a chance, but it was more than we'd had only a few seconds ago. I slapped spurs to my roan and he jumped ahead of the two horses he'd been forced to trail for so long. That horse had it in his blood to run, and it wasn't his style to stay behind any horse. That dry wash had to be at least eight feet wide where we jumped it, but all three of our horses cleared it without breaking stride. I swung hard left into a long hollow that had been formed by the runoff from the dry wash. Ann and Jamie stuck close to me like burrs on a saddle blanket, and we cut back along the hollow down into the loose sandy bottom of the dry riverbed, plunging forward at a dead run. Ann's steeldust stumbled in the soft sand, but recovered himself, picked up stride, and came a'running. We'd lost sight of the Apache coming up behind us as we cleared that gouge in the earth, but I knew they would be coming. I swung my roan hard around to the south, using a rocky gouge between the hills to work our way into them. The strides of the horses slowed to a brisk walk, but we were on hard ground, and the tracks we were leaving were few. Cresting the lowest of the hills, we cut back down behind them into a forest of jumping cactus that looked to stretch for miles. We weaved this way and that, picking our way between the prickly plants. Then I led the way back to the cluster of hills in a wide circle. I was counting more on luck than anything sensible when I cut back for those hills, and luck was something I was running hip deep in, because I found a dip between those hills that was almost completely covered by mesquite and big rocks. We didn't waste any time in getting our horses back up in there and dismounting to keep them quiet.

We sure didn't have long to wait 'til them Apache came streaming from the far side of the hills where we'd taken cover. They weren't tracking, that was sure. I reckon they were just following in the direction they figured we had to have run. It wouldn't take them long to figure out what I'd done. Then they'd be doubling back on their trail pronto, and it'd be best if we were clean out of the territory. I swung back into the saddle, and Jamie and Ann did the same without a word. There'd be time for talk later ... if there was a later. I led off, sliding my roan down the steep side of the hill, striking out again toward the west. That young fella I'd helped to get free from the Apache a couple of days back was on my mind. He'd headed west. There had to be something in that direction to draw him. In his condition he couldn't have been figuring on going far. Maybe there was a waterhole, or a place to hole up and lay low for a while. Whatever it was, I was gambling my whole pot that I'd be able to recognize it for what it was when I saw it. It was plain that wherever that young fella figured on giving them Indians the slip, it wasn't going to be out in the open.

It wasn't until we'd put a few more miles behind us, crossing the open country, that I spotted the talking smoke, threading its way up into the blueness of the sky to the southwest. I never had been much good at reading them things, but I could make out enough to know they were talking about us, and it wouldn't be too long before they had us cornered somewhere. Lifting our horses to a trot, we kept moving, the dust thick in our faces.

The air was dry, the sun hot, and my eyes felt like two hot coals rasping in my skull, but I kept looking around, staring hard as we pushed on, looking for anything that might be used for cover. I got to wondering if that young fella hadn't just lit out this way, taking a chance, just as we were doing. He could have died out here, and there wouldn't be anyone to know any different. The desert was a vast and brutal land, there wasn't any way of telling how many people just up and dropped from sight ... just never seen again.

My clothes were stiff with sweat and sand, and I knew Ann couldn't be feeling no better. The sounds of the horses' hoofs were muffled by the sand, but their tired breathing was loud enough to be heard by anybody close by. I never stopped looking around while we rode, and it didn't surprise me none to see them Apache appear on a ridge to the southwest. There just wasn't nothing else we could do but run. I slapped spurs to my roan, and let Jamie's horse have a good hard whack across the rump. Our horses were already tuckered, but they jumped into a run before those Apache had a chance to start off that ridge after us. I shucked that rifle of mine, swinging it clear of the boot as we plunged forward, the dust swirling off the desert floor around us in great clouds. I didn't reckon to be going a whole lot further. Our horses were nearly spent, and we were running out of time mighty quick. From what I could see, there were probably more than fifteen Apache in that party coming down our backs. Even a man who looked at the good side would figure we were in for a lot of trouble.

That roan I rode wanted to pull ahead even though he was getting pretty close to the end of what he had to give. Holding him back with a firm hand, I kept Jamie and Ann up ahead of me so I could try to cover our backs.

We were pushing mighty hard. The horses were all lathered up and getting weaker with each step. I was still hunting some kind of hole to crawl into to make a stand when we come up out of a dry wash and that huge, old walled ranch like to have sprung up out of the sand like a mushroom. When I first laid eyes on it I figured it for a desert mirage. Trouble was, it got bigger whilst we were coming on instead of moving back before our eyes. It was real all right, and one of the biggest I'd ever laid eyes on. The whole place was walled in like a Mexican fort, and there were several lookout towers along its length. I could feel that big roan of mine tightening up beneath me like he knew we were heading in.

The first shot sounded behind us, going good and wide, then some more followed. Those Indians were still a good ways back, but our horses were nearly spent, and they were closing the gap mighty quick. The walls were growing before us, and I could make

110

out figures of men standing along its length. They would have rifles, that much I knew. They would also be holding their fire for fear of hitting us instead of the Apache strung out behind. I had seen the same drama acted out at the fort where I had been scout. At that time there hadn't been time to saddle up horses and ride out, even if the men could have been risked. All the men inside the walls could do was wait.

Jamie was in the lead, his horse still moving strong, and him riding like he was an Apache himself. Ann was close up behind him, that little steeldust of hers still game, and I figured that even if I didn't make it, odds were they would. Their horses had been carrying about half the weight of my roan over the whole distance, and now, though the roan wasn't faltering, it was beginning to tell. His strides were coming hard, and I could almost feel his tired muscles straining for each lunge forward. Jamie and Ann were pulling ahead with nearly every stride, and those Indians were coming up fast. Bullets were filling the air thick as flies, and I felt a hot, burning pain across my ribs as I shifted in the saddle and snapped off a couple of shots behind me with my rifle. The dust was thick around me, hanging in the air from the passing of the pair of horses ahead of me.

Looking around from the Apache behind

me to Ann and Jamie in front of me, I saw that game little steeldust go down. The men up on the walls risked a couple of shots, but I didn't see if they hit anything, my eyes were locked onto where that horse fell. There must have been a hole, 'cause that horse came up on his feet almost the same instant he went down and took out at a run like he was eager to catch up with Jamie's horse, leaving Ann in the dust. Between the thunder of running hoofs and the shots going off all around, Jamie had apparently not even seen his sister's horse go down, and as far as I was concerned, it was for the best. I rammed my rifle back in its boot and stretched out my left hand to my side as I slowed my horse's stride, trying to let Ann know what I wanted.

Well, Ann was some dazed, but that girl had a head on her shoulders, and it was pretty plain to anybody with eyes in their head that we weren't going to get a second chance at this.

Ann was standing there, reaching out for me when I came up on her at a lope considerable slower than I'd been traveling, but faster than was handy. I reached down and caught her wrist, giving her a swing up, while she half crawled, half scrambled up behind me. Her arms tightened around my waist and that roan of mine took out again, acting like he was fresh from the livery. I didn't know if we were going to make it, the two of us and a near spent horse, but we were sure as hell gonna try.

Up ahead, the gates opened wide, and Jamie went on through with that steeldust heading on in like his tail was on fire. The men up on the walls were risking a few more shots as we got closer and all of a sudden it seemed like we were pulling away from the Apache behind us. A few more long strides, and we passed through that gate, that horse of mine still running all out, and me pulling him up while some men closed and barred the gate behind us.

I got that roan of mine stopped in front of a grand Mexican hacienda, and looked about myself like a man dying of thirst who has just found himself a sparkling river.

CHAPTER NINE

'We've been waiting for you almost three days now ... the desert is big amigo, but there are but few places to run.' I heard the voice before I spotted the young fella standing just inside the shade of the overhang attached to the huge Mexican hacienda. Looked to me like we found where my young friend of a couple days back had been heading when he lit out west.

113

He stepped out into the bright sunlight. He wasn't exactly a tall man, but then he wasn't what you would call short either, and his build was on the slender side. Wearing one of those white shirts with the ruffles on the front, black pants, and a sling that cradled his left arm, it was plain to see that he was taped up pretty good under the light material of his shirt. All in all, he looked a whole lot better than the last time I saw him. His black hair was brushed neatly back from his smooth forehead and his deep black eyes were filled with a devilish light. They were framed with black eyebrows arched high and balanced evenly on either side of the straight nose. His skin was much lighter than that of the other Mexicans around. It wasn't a whole lot darker than mine, and I was lighter than most folks.

'The last time we met,' he said with a grin, 'we didn't have time to exchange names. I am Carlos Otero, and this'—he waved his good arm about him—'is my father's ranchero.'

'The name's Logan,' I said quickly, 'Matt Logan ... Matt's fine.' Behind me I could feel Ann shifting her weight and sliding off my horse to the ground. That roan of mine was blowing pretty good and I followed Ann's example, stepping down from the saddle.

'Pedro,' Carlos called to one of the men

walking in our direction, 'take their horses and see that they are cared for as though they were my father's.'

Pedro, a tall, lanky man with a drooping mustache and dark, sad eyes nodded shortly and without a word, gathered up the horses, moving off with them.

Carlos was looking at Ann with the eye of a man appreciating a pretty woman, and while his eyes held hers, there was something more. He grinned at me. 'I can see why you didn't follow me back there. She is worth the risk you took.'

Gesturing toward where Jamie had left Pedro and was heading in our direction, I said a mite uncomfortable like, 'He's the one we went after.'

'No matter,' Carlos chuckled. 'You would not have gone after him if it had not been for her.'

Ann blushed, and there wasn't nothing I could say without getting myself in trouble with someone, so I kept my mouth shut. Looked to me like he made a hit with her right off. Them looking at each other that away brought back to me the magic that sprung up between my wife and myself the day we met. Jamie got over to us about the time an older man appeared beneath the overhang next to Carlos.

Stepping from the stone patio, he extended his hand. 'I am Don Manuel

115

Otero. You will have to forgive my inconsiderate son who leaves the man who saved his life standing in front of our home.' Don Manuel lifted my shirt where the Apache bullet had sliced through the cloth and the skin beneath, 'Bleeding,' he added.

Don Manuel Otero was a short, squared off man with coal black hair that was graying a mite in the front, and a full beard that was streaked with white. He spoke with a voice that was soft, cultured, and thick with the accent of his native Mexico. A voice that was filled with pride when he spoke of his son even when that young fella stepped out of line. He wore a broad smile that split his dark face, and brought tiny lines to the corners of his eyes. His eyes were the darkest black I'd ever come across, except maybe for his son, Carlos, standing right behind him.

'You must come inside,' Don Manuel said real friendly like, 'my house is your house.' A mite nervous, I kind of looked around behind me. 'What about them Apache, Don Manuel, it kind'a seems to me that I brought you a passel of trouble.'

He chuckled dryly as he looked over his shoulder toward the walls. 'Do not trouble yourself, my friend. We have fought them many times before. They will not attack right away. First, they must think about it. Then, if they choose to attack, my men will drive them off.' As he kept on talking, he herded

116

us all inside ahead of him. 'The walls are six feet thick, and there are double gates. We are as safe here as in a town farther north ... perhaps safer.'

We stepped out of the hot sun into a huge entrance hall, the like of which I never expected to see this side of Mexico City. There was a comfortable coolness about the room. It showed that the desert sun could be shut out if a man put his mind to it. It was high ceilinged, with massive front doors. There were portraits on the walls, and the furniture looked to have been fetched all the way from Europe. From there, Don Manuel led the way into a living room that looked big enough for bronc riding. There was a rock fireplace that took up most of the west wall. More pictures hung on the walls, some of the desert, a few of beautiful horses, and one in particular that hung above the fireplace. It was a picture of a woman, and what a woman she was. Her skin was light, and looked to be the color of honey. Beautiful blue eyes like velvet seemed to stare out of the portrait right at a man. They were large, round, and framed by eyebrows the same honey color as her hair, and as delicately shaped as a bird's wing. Her nose was small and straight, and her lips softly bow shaped. A hint of a smile sort of hung about the lips of the slender young woman in the portrait and it spread a feeling of happiness over the whole room.

Don Manuel had caught me staring at the portrait, but he was a man to make others feel at ease. 'That was my wife. Most people who come to my home for the first time stare at it. She was a very beautiful woman. The painting of her was done more than eighteen years ago. It was finished just a few months before an Apache arrow killed her.'

When a body looked at that painting, it wasn't hard to tell who Carlos took after. There was a lot of his ma in him. I glanced over at Ann, and it was plain to see that she was feeling a mite uneasy. Women sure are funny. She was used to the Eastern ways, and their fine houses, but here she felt out of place. If I guessed right, it was because of them clothes she was wearing, and the dust we were packing from some mighty long days on the trail.

'Perhaps the young lady would like to freshen up.' That Don Manuel was a right canny man. There wasn't much he missed, from what I could see.

Ann's face lit up at his words. 'Yes, I would, thank you,' she said quietly. Her eyes hung on Carlos and his on her.

'And you,' Don Manuel said to Jamie. 'I am sure you would like something to eat.'

That Jamie was a growing boy, and he didn't have to be asked twice when it came to food. A pair of Mexican women, house servants appeared, and Ann and Jamie left the room in their care.

It was just about then that Carlos came back into the room with a man I hadn't seen before. It was plain to me he was from north of the border, but tanned dark. There wasn't no mistaking that here was a man who could take care of himself.

'This is Jake Smith,' Carlos informed me. 'He's our doctor out here. My father bribed him off a wagon train headed for California a few years ago.'

Jake gave me a faint smile and gestured for me to sit down in one of the heavily carved chairs near the fireplace. He opened my shirt where the bullet had nicked me and started cleaning the wound. Jake wasn't a man who wasted words.

'I'll be around if you need me for anything else,' Jake said as he finished bandaging the burn the bullet had left when he left the room. Seemed like Jake just didn't have anything else to say.

Carlos dropped into the massive chair across from mine. 'You'll be staying on a few days.' The mellow firmness in Carlos's voice made it hard for a body to argue with him. 'Sides, the past few days on the trail had been hard on us and the horses. All of us could use a rest and some good grub. Those Apache right outside the gate also helped me make up my mind to stay.

I stretched to keep from stiffening up and nodded. 'A day or two anyhow,' I told him.

'Good,' Don Manuel said crisply. 'We don't have visitors out here very often.' His smile showed through that wiry beard of his. 'When we do, we don't like to let them get away too soon.' Don Manuel sat himself down on one of those sofas with heavy curved legs, and broad wooden arms.

'I've been wondering what fortune it was that brought you all the way out here,' Carlos said to me as I settled back in that overstuffed chair, easing tired muscles.

'That's a mighty long story, start to finish, even longer than what I know.' I was starting to relax, knowing the safety of the adobe walls surrounded me, and was beginning to feel like I'd been dragged over a mess of rocks, cactus, and brush. It'd been a considerable time since I'd had some good sack time. 'You'd do better to ask Ann,' I went on, 'but what it boils down to is we come out here after her brother, Jamie.' From wherever the cooking was being done, the air carried the smell of something I hadn't come across in some time. It was chicken. I'd been living on beef, beans and biscuits so long, I'd almost forgotten what chicken smelled like.

Don Manuel was looking at me closely. 'It is a long way to my Rancho, and I know there are no others near.' He sighed. 'It has been many years since I was young and strong enough to attempt such as what you have done.'

It didn't seem like an answer was expected, so I just kept my mouth shut, and my foot out of it. It wasn't more'n a couple of seconds later when Ann appeared at the head of the stairs and started down. She'd changed out of her trail clothes and was wearing full Mexican skirts, and a bright colored blouse with short sleeves that are sort of puffy near the shoulder. That auburn hair of hers was loose, like that first time I saw her on the streets of Tucson. She was a vision, all right, and the way she moved in them skirts, it looked like she was floating down them stairs. Carlos caught sight of her out of the corner of his eye, jumped up, and crossed the room to offer her his arm before I could even give the matter proper consideration. It didn't matter none anyhow. From what I could see Carlos had himself a case on her, and aside from that, I was old enough to be that girl's father ... well, almost. What topped it was the way Ann was looking at him. There was a softness in her eyes, and I reckon I knew what was coming. She was looking at him like a woman thinking serious about a man.

Her looking like she did, got me to thinking how I looked. It figured to be some worse than when I drifted off the trail into

Tucson before I got hauled into this thing. Seemed like those old jeans I wore got thinner with every trip out. My old brown shirt was stiff with dust and sweat. It had been ripped and patched in more places than I could remember. Being a man of limited resources, getting only what I could work for with my own two hands, that old black vest stayed with me, getting more scars in the leather, and more dust in the cracks. The battered brown hat I wore fared no better. To top it off, there was dust and grit all through my hair which was getting shaggier with every passing day. And, if a body looked close enough, he'd likely see the dust coating my eyeballs. They itched and watered, giving me no peace. Little clouds of dust fell away from my buckskin chaps as I stood up.

'Reckon I'd best knock some of the dust off before I sit up to table with you folks. This sure ain't no trail drive.' Don Manuel and these folks knew what it was to come in off the desert with dust hanging on everything you owned, but it just plain wasn't good manners to be setting up to table like that when a man could avoid it. Especially in a place like this.

I'd loosened my holster so it was no longer tied down to my leg. Leather slapped leather as I walked and my boots made a hollow thumping sound as I crossed the room and followed Don Manuel's directions to the guest rooms.

CHAPTER TEN

Jamie had been at dinner. Britches and a shirt had been found for him to wear, but I noticed that he kept the moccasins. It was an easy thing for me to understand that. A body got used to walking in moccasins, it was right hard to go back to boots. Moccasins were a sight more comfortable.

Ann and Carlos looked to have themselves a lot to talk about so I got up early from the table, telling them I hadn't had a night's sleep for nigh unto a week. That part was true enough, and I was fixing to try out the softness of their beds pronto, but first there was something else that needed tending to.

I made my way along the dark stairway and halls without candle or lamp to light my way, feeling at home in the quiet darkness. Inside my room, I lit a lamp, and smiled, thinking of Ann as I blew out the match. She and Carlos were hitting it off right fine. Ol' Don Manuel must have liked the idea himself 'cause I heard him offer to take Jamie out to see the stables before I even started up the stairs. Leaving a lamp lit on the table near the door, I crossed the room to where my gear was lying on one of them big wooden chests where folks store blankets and the like. I picked up my bedroll and opened it up on the bed. I was of a mind to check that shotgun Turk'd loaned me back in Tucson. That thing was a mighty strange-looking weapon, and up to now I'd favored my rifle, but the rest of this trip was shaping up to make the part we'd already traveled look like a Sunday school picnic, and I wanted that gun handy. It had a small leather boot, smaller than a rifle's and larger than a holster, that could be strapped to a saddle. Next time we pulled out, it was going to be where I could put my hands on it in a hurry. That gun was like a cannon. Kind of cut off on the stock, and cut off on the barrels, it cut a wide swatch when a body let her loose. It was a revolver, packing four shots to boot. I dug out some of the oversized shells from my gear and filled the empty chambers of the gun. Snapping the gun back together, I just kind of held it for a couple of minutes before laying it on the chest.

Peeling out of my duds, I laid that little hideout gun I carried nestled up against my belly on the chest with the shotgun. Didn't reckon to be needing it for a spell. I was getting ready to catch some shut-eye, but couldn't stop thinking about our situation. If a body could have seen me, he'd a said I was looking mighty grim. We'd gotten this far, but we were still a good three or four days' hard ride out of Tucson. There was still a lot of country to cover, and all of it right unfriendly. It wasn't even a sure thing it'd be friendly when we reached Tucson. If Bull Morton and his boys didn't run into us before we got there, they would sure as hell be waiting for us when we got there. If Turk knew what was going on, he'd sure enough be out on the trail with a buffalo gun to sort of even things out a mite. Of course, I didn't have no way of telling what was going on back in town, but it didn't seem to me that Turk would have any way of knowing what was going on in the desert either. Piling into that bed, I felt the crisp coolness of sheets beneath me, and drifted off to sleep almost the instant I stretched out.

Seemed like only a few minutes had passed since I'd closed my eyes when I came awake with a start, staring up at the ceiling. For a few seconds I laid quiet, it was best to let things sort themselves out. The room felt different than when I sacked out. Hours had passed, I was sure of that. I looked out the open window. Near dawn I'd say. I rolled out of bed, stepped into my pants, and buckled on my gun as fast as one could follow the other. Padding across the room in bare feet I had me a better looksee out that window. There was folks stirring down below. This was a big ranch, that should be

125

natural at this hour, but there was something wrong ... something nagging at me. There was much more excitement below, much more tension in the air than there would have been with sleepy cowhands rolling out for a day's work. I padded back to my bed and pulled my boots on, then threw my shirt on without bothering to button it, and grabbed my rifle from where it stood against the wall as I went out the door.

Moving down the hall with long, quiet strides, my unbuttoned shirt flapped around me as I walked. Ann's door swung open as I came across from it, and she stood framed in the doorway, fully dressed. It wasn't them clothes she'd borrowed last night either, it was her trail clothes that she wore.

'What's wrong?' Her voice was low, urgent.

'Ain't sure,' I told her in a whisper, 'but I got me a pretty good idea.'

I could almost feel them large eyes of hers staring at me in the dim light. 'What?' she asked.

'Apache.' I lit out down them stairs, leaving her standing in the hall. For once she showed some good sense and didn't try to follow.

The door remained closed as I passed by Jamie's room. Reckon I knew pretty much what that boy'd been through, but I couldn't help wondering. That'd been his brother the

Indians had killed. Had Jamie seen it? I didn't rightly see how he could have missed it. Probably hadn't been much time for thinking since then, and certainly not during the past couple of days since I'd pulled him out of that camp. Odds were, once that boy got himself some time to be pondering on the past, he'd be having nightmares to make a body's hair stand on end.

Outside, I stood in the dark shadow cast by the overhang attached to the house and let my rifle rest in the crook of my arm as I buttoned my shirt. Beyond my patch of shadow, folks were moving about mighty quick, like there was something that needed tending to, and it couldn't wait. There was a lot to see in the dimly lit enclosure. Men were moving up to the walls, and all were carrying rifles. They moved in silence and without any lanterns to light their paths.

'You are truly a light sleeper, amigo.' Carlos appeared beside me like a ghost and gazed out across the courtyard. 'Sure am,' I chuckled softly as though at a private joke. 'Keeps a man healthy.' I took me a quick look around the compound that was already brightening with the oncoming dawn. 'Apache?' I turned toward Carlos, and it was more of a statement of fact than a question.

He shrugged and nodded. 'My father was fairly certain they would not attack by night. Dawn seems to hold some fascination for them.'

I nodded, and my eyes kept moving. It had been a rare thing to see the Apache attack by night during my scouting days. I'd heard tell somewheres that they believed if they were killed at night their spirit would wander forever in darkness. That had never made much sense to me, but who is to say that what other folks believe can be any more wrong than what I believe?

My hat was on my head as I started across the open, Carlos by my side, and I didn't even remember picking it up when I left my room. Got to be a habit like most things in life. I bounded up the stairs to the ledge inside the wall two at a time, and Carlos kept right up there with me. The open country stretched out below us. I couldn't see anything moving, but the feeling was there just like Don Manuel must have felt it. The sky was brightening by stages, the morning clouds separating before the sun's onslaught. Knowing what was coming, I tensed and could feel my muscles bunching up.

'How'd your daddy get these walls up before the Apache could wipe him out anyway?' I threw the question sideways, not really glancing in Carlos's direction.

'I was not yet born,' Carlos told me, 'but some of the men who were here when my father first came said he and my mother, and the best fighting men he could find, came

128

when most of the Apache were summering in the mountains north of here. There were some fights, of course, but by the time the main tribe got back, the walls were nearly finished. Even now the vaqueros who watch the herds fight more than herd cattle. That's what I was doing when they ran me down. I got a little too far out and they cut me off. It was lucky for me you came when you did.'

The sun had come up on the eastern horizon when that first shot came whistling in from far out in the brush. Me and Carlos hunkered down behind that adobe wall and let the burning arrow pass on by. Neither one of us bothered to throw any lead out that way without no target to aim at. Second and third arrows followed the first, but everybody just stayed put, and didn't pay 'em much mind. They were all striking the dirt inside the walls. There wasn't much inside the compound that would burn anyways, Don Manuel had expertly seen to that. Them arrows kept a'coming, and Don Manuel's boys stayed where they was. Some of them almost looked bored. I glanced around from one to another of the men I could see from where I was, and you didn't have to be particularly smart to be able to tell Don Manuel had himself a pretty tough bunch of hands. They'd all been through it before, and figured on going through it again. That was what they were paid for.

'Here they come!' A voice shouted from somewhere down the line, his last word drowned out by the explosion of gunfire.

I got up on one knee and slipped my rifle barrel through a loophole while I had me a look at what was going on below. Seemed like there was Apache all over the place, the way they kept bobbing up from behind rocks, and mesquite. One or two would jump up, running toward the walls whilst the rest gave him cover, and just as we'd get our rifles swung around, that one or two would disappear and a couple more would start up. I'd seen the like before, more times than I cared to remember. So had these men of Don Manuel. They weren't firing wildly, they were waiting, as I was, for a clear shot. Enough of those Apache down there had rifles to keep all of us looking sharp. Lead was whistling around our ears and scarring those thick adobe walls that protected us.

Carlos was packing the same kind of rifle as me, a Winchester '73, carrying seventeen shots, and he knew how to use it. I seen him wing a couple, and when he missed clean, it wasn't by enough to split a hair.

Me, I snapped off a few shots where I saw some of them Apache take to cover, then settled down to picking my target. I watched one of them jump up, run a few strides, and take to cover again behind a fold in the earth. That fold ran a few feet in either direction so

I took a chance on which way he'd roll and shifted my aim. When he come up again, he was right in my sights, and my shot took him square. He fell backward behind that dip where he'd been taking cover, and I didn't figure he'd be popping up again real soon.

Out of the corner of my eye, I saw one of the men catch a slug and go down. That Doc Don Manuel had bribed off that wagon train showed up out of nowheres, bandaged that fella, and dragged him down off the catwalk to the house. He was muttering something that sounded a mite uncomplimentary to himself as he passed by us, carrying the wounded man slung over one shoulder. Those were the first words I'd heard ol' Jake say without 'em being pulled out of him. Didn't seem to me that he was too fond of them Apache.

Then, all of a sudden, the attack broke. I leaned up against the inside of the wall and started to slide down to sit on my heels and reload while Carlos started to straighten up to have himself a better look below. Reckon from where he was he couldn't see what I had. Six Apache had gone to ground a mite beyond the walls, and I hadn't seen 'em lite out. He figured them for having pulled back for a spell, and most times he'd a' been right. Trouble was, this time he wasn't, so I just naturally reached out and tripped him, flattened him on the wooden walk about a

131

second before six or eight slugs came flying into 'dobe around us. Reddish-tan dust settled down on top of us as the bullets chipped some of the adobe loose from the top of the wall. Carlos had looked some surprised when I flipped him on his back like a defeated desert tortoise, but now he shook some of the dust from his black hair and gave a low whistle.

'Now I know you'd have better sense than that,' I said past my rifle barrel, 'if you knew we still had company.' I gestured toward the low ridge where the Apache were still holed up.

Chuckling softly, Carlos grinned at me while still brushing the dust from his clothes and hair. He picked up his rifle and sat on his heels facing me. 'You are quick, amigo, very quick.'

Reckoning he didn't expect me to answer him, I just kept on reloading and got set for the next attack. The Apache would probably come a couple times more before they decided to give up or try something else. We'd done them some hurt. Only one of our men had picked up a slug, and I know there were three or four of them packing lead. It was an unusual situation. Usually, it was the Apache who managed to come up with the advantage. Mostly, it was them who lost only one man to the enemies' three or four. For a change we were on the high ground surrounded by walls that they hadn't managed to penetrate in better than eighteen years. That didn't mean it couldn't happen, just gave them Apache something to think about.

By nature I wasn't a sitting man, and I could be right patient when need be. Thinking on getting back to Tucson was getting me some nervous, and I had me a gut feeling them Apache were right upset about me stealing one of their captives right from under their noses. They didn't take kindly to folks riding into their country, and stirring things up. It made 'em look a mite foolish and they didn't take kindly to that neither. It didn't seem to me that they meant to give up on us. I'd fought 'em, tracked 'em, and crossed trails with 'em long enough to know that. Even if they called off the attack on Don Manuel's fort, I figured them to be waiting for us, somewhere along the trail, when we left. And if that was what they were planning on, I didn't see no point in letting them get set for us.

Standing up, I stayed kind of hunched over and started back down the wooden stairs. Quickly, Carlos motioned for one of the other men to take over our position, and came along behind me.

'There is something on your mind, amigo?' He held his rifle by the trigger guard, and then let the barrel rest on his shoulder. I felt like them soft, black eyes of his were boring right through me.

I nodded. 'We're clearing out. They're going to just sit out there, waiting 'til we do. Them Apache get mighty determined when they figure a body has made fools of them,' I went on, 'and it looks like I done it twice lately. When I got you loose, and when I took Jamie. Don't reckon they hold me in too high regard, and knowing them like I do, I don't figure they'll give up 'til I'm clean out of the territory.'

Carlos gave me a hard look and shook his head. 'You are loco! They will kill you all before you get a hundred yards outside the gate.'

Starting toward the house, I shrugged at Carlos's statement. 'I know this kind of country up, down, and sideways, and I ain't been nailed yet. 'Sides,' I went on hopefully, 'I don't figure a smart man like your daddy would have left this place with only one way out.'

Carlos started to say something, but his father appeared from out of nowhere. 'You are right, senõr, there is another way out. It has not been used in all the years we have been here.' His voice was calm and soft. It sure beat all how that man could move with all the silence of his enemies, the Apache.

'Our horses are rested,' I told him, 'and them Apache are going to be on your back as long as we're here. Plain fact of the matter is, we got to leave sometime, and the way I see it, the sooner the better.'

'There is logic in what you say,' Don Manuel agreed. 'I will send some riders with you.'

I shook my head. 'Much obliged, but we can move faster alone, and a lot of riders would be easier to spot than just three.'

Don Manuel frowned and spread his hands helplessly. 'It seems there is nothing I can do to help you as you helped my son.' Them black eyes of his held mine, never faltering.

'I am going with you,' Carlos broke in. He took off the sling that he still wore, and worked his arm up and down. 'You cannot dissuade me, senõr, so do not try ... it was my life you saved, and it is my debt to pay.'

I was sort of hoping Don Manuel would have something of his own to say on the subject, but all the while I knew he wouldn't. 'I will see that everything is made ready for you to leave,' he said quietly, and disappeared before I could say anything more. I kind of suspicioned that Carlos had a mite more on his mind than paying back a debt he owed. Ann was a real pretty girl, and Carlos wasn't a man to give up easy.

CHAPTER ELEVEN

Don Manuel didn't waste no time in getting everything ready for us to lite out. Didn't seem like he was a man to waste time in anything he did. Ann hadn't looked too happy about going out there in the thick of them Apache again, but we'd spent enough time together on the trail for her to know I didn't do my talking just to stir up the wind. She figured if we were clearing out there had to be a good reason, and helped get things ready. Don Manuel led the way inside, through the huge living room to where the second way out was hidden. He pulled one of them tapestries off the wall, and behind it was a door of heavy timbers five feet wide by what looked like better'n nine feet high. I couldn't help staring. It just never crossed my mind to find Don Manuel's path of retreat leading right through his living room.

Smiling, he threw the heavy tapestry to one side. 'You are wondering why I chose to put the door here instead of outside somewhere?' Don Manuel explained simply. 'This door leads right through the wall to the outside. When we built this hacienda, it was designed so that if the walls were ever broken through, and the Apache were overrunning the yard, we could fall back into the house

136

with some horses, and slip out the back way.' He smiled grimly. 'This is my home, senõr. I would fight to the death for it if there was a chance of winning, but I always fully intended to live here ... not to die foolishly here.'

Made sense to me. A man had to know when to fight and when to make tracks if he was figuring on living very long in these parts. I've done my share of hightailing it in Indian country. When a sensible man sees a war party of ten or twelve Indians coming down on him, he just naturally clears out, and he'd be moving mighty fast.

One of Don Manuel's men brought in the horses, their hoofs thumping hollowly on the wooden floor. The three we rode in looked well rested and eager for the trail. The fourth one was one of the hardest muscled, cleanest limbed animals I'd come across in some time of wandering. Reckon he was the best Don Manuel's place had to offer. I couldn't see him giving anything less than that to his son. That roan of mine nickered and reached out his head to be stroked. He'd been brushed and tended to like he was a show horse. That roan would be carrying the heaviest load on the trail, for I was not a small man. Having had him since he was a green, half-broke horse, I knew him to have more heart than any two horses I'd ever owned. If I was a betting man, I'd put my money on that roan before any of the other three horses there, including the one Don Manuel had for his son.

Don Manuel broke into my thoughts. 'When the door is opened you must leave quickly ... it is concealed on the outside by a covering of adobe filling the cracks and smoothing it into a part of the wall. The Apache have not known that door exists. If you are caught...' His voice dropped to a whisper, but I caught the expression on his face as he looked toward his son.

Shots sounded again from out front as I stepped into the saddle. Ann, Jamie, and Carlos did the same as I glanced back over my shoulder to where the sounds of the fighting were again growing louder.

'Now is the time,' Don Manuel said urgently. 'There is extra food in your saddlebags, and I have ordered the extra canteens on your saddles. There is nothing more I can do. Go now, while my men are giving them something to think about out front.'

Three of Don Manuel's men pushed and sweated working that heavy door loose. When it finally swung open, the adobe dust filtering down around the frame, I was already halfway through, heading for the shelter of a clump of mesquite. Ann and Jamie were up close behind me, and Carlos brought up the rear. Carlos and me both rode with our rifles out. The sounds of gunfire thundered between the rolling hills, and even as Carlos's horse came clear of the door, his father's men were pulling it closed again. Looked like we were on our own again, heading on out into open desert.

After making sure everyone was close, I started out, picking my way along, keeping anything I could between us and them Apache. I breathed a mite easier when we come across another dry wash and moved on into it. It would shield us from view for several hundred yards, and if our luck held and we weren't seen, it should give us a better chance than I'd hoped for. I knew too well that them Apache would find our tracks outside them walls. It wouldn't take them long either. They were prowlers, always looking around, and they wouldn't miss the fresh tracks of four horses. They'd be more interested in four riders alone than in Don Manuel's fort, so they'd be following along behind like dogs on a trail. Our best hope was in putting as much distance between us and them as we could.

An easy trail was what I was wishful for, though in these parts that wasn't something a man very often came upon. There'd be no resting for quite a spell. The horses were fresh, and I wasn't figuring on losing any time putting that territory behind me.

Carlos was something I hadn't figured on.

I'm a lone riding man. Never have been too fond of the idea of lookin' out after other folks. It puts too much weight on a man, being responsible for another's life. Out here there was usually problems enough keeping your own hide in one piece without hunting more trouble. Carlos was a crack shot with that rifle though, and of that much I was glad. He'd been brung up in this country, the 'Pache pounding at the front door, Mexican banditos pounding at the back. There would be no hesitation in him to shoot if need be. Ann and Jamie were another worry. Ann could shoot, that much I knew. Trouble was she didn't have much trail experience. When a showdown came, she could be the one to sort of hang back, and that could be hell for us all.

Behind some low hills we come out of that wash, and I kept the horses to a walk, trying to keep the dust down as we moved. If them 'Pache spotted a dust cloud, they'd be sure to take it into their heads to have themselves a look-see, and that was something we surely didn't need right now. From time to time I glanced back over my shoulder, looking past those who rode with me, and concentrating on the changing country around us. It was right uncanny sometimes, the way them Apache could just appear right out of nowhere, and I aimed to be ready.

For a time I'd been heading north and a

hair west of Don Manuel's place, keeping up against the back of those hills. We were already quite a stretch west and south of Tucson, and I figured we couldn't risk any more distance than what we already had, so I cut due north. I was remembering what Turk had been saying back in town about the Flannigan spread. With a little luck, we just might run across it. If not, that would put us that much closer to Tucson. Smiling grimly to myself, I got to thinking about Turk waiting back in Tucson. He'd be climbing the walls by now, figuring us all for dead. Me and Ann leastways, him not knowing about Jamie and Carlos.

I took my hat off and dragged a sleeve across my forehead. That sun was getting higher in the sky, and hotter all the time. Seemed like when a man was traveling in the desert the sun climbed to noon faster, and stayed there longer than anywhere else. Putting my hat back on my head, I let my eyes wander back to the front. I remembered Turk saying the Flannigan spread was a couple of days' ride from Tucson. The way I figured it that would put us at least four days out. It wasn't a pleasant thought, but it was a fact that had to be faced. We were far enough away from the ranch now ... I lifted my roan to a trot. The others followed. Glancing back I noticed Carlos having himself a good look around. He sure was no

141

tenderfoot, and it gave me some comfort to know them coal black eyes of his wouldn't be missing much in the rocks and sand that spread out in all directions around us. Carlos had him some first hand experience about what it meant to tangle with the Apache and lose. He wasn't completely healed from that experience yet, and it was in me to hope that wouldn't be slowing him down none.

We pushed hard most of that day, skirting low hills, riding in the concealment of dry washes, and crossing the glaring white of dry lakes. The sun rose and set on a sky a washed out blue, bearing no clouds on its winds to break the sun's glare. We made dry camp, and had no fire. It didn't seem like the next day was going to be any better than this, or the two days after to come. When a man was in a town, or in the high up mountains with nothing but himself, three or four days didn't seem like much, but here it seemed like years.

Ann was digging in the saddlebags for some grub and Carlos was standing watch partway up the hill behind us when Jamie came up and dropped down on the ground across from me, cross-legged, Indian style. He stared at me with them big brown eyes of his, never wavering in his gaze. Round and trusting as all get out, them eyes of his made me a mite nervous. His skin had been darkened considerable by the desert sun, but

142

there were still plenty of freckles sprinkled across his nose and cheeks. His light brown hair was long and shaggy and he was looking at me out of a little boy's face, right down to the up-turned nose. Trouble was, that light that shone in them eyes didn't belong to no little boy. A mite past twelve was just plain too young to have to grow up, but what had been done couldn't be undone. The gun Turk had loaned me was in my hands, and I was checkin' it over to make sure it was clean and loaded when needed. Jamie watched in silence, his long legs crossed before him.

Something was rattling around in that head of his, of that I was sure. When he finally spoke his voice was low and solemn. 'You don't really think we'll make it back, do you?'

The question kind of caught me unawares. I stopped fooling with that gun and looked over at him. His face was troubled and still. 'I don't rightly know, Jamie,' I told him honestly. Never did figure it was right to lie to a kid just 'cause he was a kid.

Jamie stared at me for a long time. He dropped his eyes to the sand, idly using a stick to draw in it, then returned his gaze to me. 'Mr Logan,' he said, his voice low, his tone measured. 'You have to promise me . . . if the Apache come, and you can't stop them, that you'll shoot Ann.'

Now I've never been a father, never even

143

been around kids much, but I figured I had to say something to him. Gesturing for him to come closer, I set that gun I'd been cleaning aside. He moved over and sat beside me whilst I sort of mulled over in my mind what I was gonna say.

'Jamie,' I began, 'you know your sister come a long way to find you. She took an almighty lot of chances just to get this far.' I paused. 'Now don't you think a person who's done all that, has the right to decide for herself what you're asking me?'

Once again Jamie dropped his gaze to the sand. 'I know the Apache,' he said slowly, 'I'm ... I'm only thinking about Ann.'

Looking right into Jamie's eyes, I nodded slowly. 'Reckon I already know that, Jamie. You growed up a lot in these few months, but pretty soon you'll find out that no matter how much growing up a man does, there's always some further he has to go. Men are kind of funny critters,' I told him, 'you have to learn to figure them. Like this thing with Ann. If them 'Pache were overrunning us and there didn't look to be no other choice ... say I did what you said and shot her. Then at the last second the army shows up and it turns out I didn't have to do it. Living with myself would be hell, but it probably wouldn't last long 'cause folks would take it into their heads that it was murder and I'd likely be strung up pronto.' Glancing up, I

144

saw Ann was still busy on the far side of the camp. 'On the other hand,' I told him, 'if I done what I figured to be right and them Indians killed us all and it was ever found what happened, folks would claim it was the kindest thing to do.' I looked over at him and found his eyes staring back into mine. 'A man has to meet things as they come, and do what he figures is right, 'cause it ain't nobody else but his own life that he's living. You understand what I'm saying?'

A mite puzzled, Jamie thought on it for a spell then nodded. 'It's sort of like what my pa told me about not jumping to conclusions.' He said the last word kind of slow. 'That's what my pa called it anyway.'

I sighed. Some folks could say things a lot clearer'n me. Sometimes it seemed like most folks could. 'Your pa was right. A man should think on things, that's why he has a brain.'

Jamie fell silent beside me, and I looked up to let my eyes wander through the rapidly gathering darkness. It was quiet, and a bright quarter moon hung low in the sky. The horses were making soft animal sounds a short distance away. They were peaceful sounds, there was nothing about to spook them. Ann came up, gave Jamie and me some hardtack and biscuits, then picked her way up the hill to take some to Carlos where he stood watch.

'Do you live in Tucson, Mr Logan?' Jamie asked me.

Refocusing my thoughts on the boy beside me, I shook my head. 'No, I do a lot of wandering, Jamie. Don't stay too long in one spot.'

'I don't want to go back East,' Jamie said flatly, 'but I know Ann does, and so I guess we will. I wish we could stay ... in Tucson maybe.'

'You best get your bedroll and get some rest,' I said avoiding saying anything about his last statement. 'There's a sight of country we have to get across yet.' That boy had gotten himself a real liking for these parts, and it seemed to me that taking him out of them wouldn't be doing him no favor.

I watched Jamie go for his bedroll, then returned my gaze to the wide open desert that surrounded us. For now it was empty. Empty and quiet, but the Apache would come. There was no question about their coming. I'd spent enough time in this country to know that for a fact. The question that tugged at the back of my mind was when.

CHAPTER TWELVE

It was still dark as cinder, but it was coming

on toward morning, and I figured it wouldn't be long 'til we pulled out again. I'd taken over the watch from Carlos close to midnight, and nothing had been stirring all night. Just about the time I was ready to cross the first night off, and start to worrying about the day stretching out before us, I spotted a shadow slipping over the ground some ways out from our camp. Now I stood enough watches and kept an eye on enough chaparral and cactus to know trouble when it was heading my way. That little cannon, half shotgun was with me, and that was one weapon that didn't need to be aimed. Just point the thing, then pull the trigger was all it took. I hefted it in one hand and slipped on down the hill where I'd been standing watch. Some trouble was crawling up our backs, and it was time the rest knew about it.

Rousing Carlos first, I warned him to silence. He come up off'a that bedroll touchier'n a teased snake. With sign language I let him know what was coming. He slipped off toward the horses, his bedroll wadded in one hand, his rifle at the ready in the other. If them Apache got our horses we'd be in a real bad way, and everybody knew it, including them Indians. There'd been no campfire, so they'd found us by chance or by some mistake we'd made. There hadn't been a lot of time to hide our trail. Too much out in the open, and too few guns among us, we couldn't stand and fight if we wanted to.

The instant I touched her Ann came awake, and I saw her eyes widen in surprise as she looked beyond my shoulder. Without no hesitating at all I jumped up and stepped sideways. I read that look in her eyes real clear and wasn't surprised none when I met that Indian head on as he come across our camp like a phantom. A rock-hard fist caught him in the belly as I dropped to one knee, rolling him over my shoulder with his own momentum. Ann pushed Jamie and they jumped to their feet, Ann snatching up the rifle she kept close beside her. Over by the horses I heard a rifle crack. Carlos was having some trouble of his own, and I was hoping there weren't too many for him to handle.

A second Indian came for me while the first had come to his feet about as quick as a cat. Ann came up behind him and laid the butt of that rifle across his skull. He folded up without a sound and the other one disappeared into the desert. No further shots came from Carlos's direction. It all happened so fast, I still held my gun unused in my hand.

I didn't figure them few Indians could be a part of that bunch that hit Don Manuel's place. There were too few of them, and the attack wasn't really a whole-hearted effort on their part. Must have been some raiding band returning to the mountains that stumbled on our camp by chance and figured us for an easy kill. Seemed like only three or four were in the band. The attack had been much too swift and short for anything else.

Carlos brought the horses up before I had a chance to go to him. He passed a few words with Ann, low, comforting words, his lips close to her ear. He kissed her lightly on the cheek when he figured me to be too busy to notice. Ann smiled at him kind of soft, then turned to her horse. We threw our supplies together and mounted up. Those shots Carlos exchanged with the Apache would have been heard for miles. If that bunch from Don Manuel's was out there somewheres looking for us, them shots would bring them a'running.

The horses started out at a brisk trot for a ways, then we slowed them to a walk to rest them, and a little later lifted them to a trot again. Nothing but distance was what I wanted between us and the place where we'd camped the night. Dawn came quickly, sooner than I cared to see it. It lit up the sky with hot yellow and blazed down on us with a brassy glare. A hot wind had come up, kicking up the sand and dust around us, making the air almost unbearable to breathe. If it weren't for the feeling of suffocation, I would have been almost glad, for the wind would help cover what tracks we left. Trouble was, I had felt the desert get like this before, and more than once. There was a storm in the air, the kind we'd want no part of. I'd been through a few sand storms in my time, and that was exactly what we were heading into now.

It's right wearing on a man to be always looking over his shoulder, while at the same time trying to figure what was coming next. Heat waves were starting to come up off the ground. Carlos come up beside me from behind and looked about nervously.

'Trouble never comes singly, my friend,' he said meaningfully as he dragged a sleeve across his forehead. The feel of the desert was something he was acquainted with too. 'You have any ideas?'

I threw him a half smile and shrugged. 'We could try an' out run it, that is if we knew where it was coming from. From where I sit, it looks to me like we're gonna have to find some place to turtle in and wait it out.'

Pretty well out in the open, there was nothing much 'sides mesquite and cactus to break the force of that wind that was coming. We cut off to the east and put our horses to a gallop. Far off in the distance the sky had turned a dusty yellow. The sun shone steadily, but it looked to be a hazy blur in the sky. The air was still, and felt sort of crackling like. Then Carlos pointed out a cluster of rocks ahead. They were clustered up against the foot of some low hills like they was huddled together for each other's comfort. We put the horses to a run, heading them for the rocks for all we were worth. Them horses didn't need no urging for they had already caught the scent of the coming storm, and were eager to run.

By the time we reached them rocks there wasn't anything stirring ... not a bird flying, not so much as a lizard slipping through the sand at our feet as we dismounted. The air was stifling, suffocating, and far off in the distance was the tiny sound that would soon become a shrieking howl and block everything else from the world. Carlos and me, we worked like madmen, hobbling the horses, tying them fast to keep them from lunging free, and trying to run ahead of the storm when there was nowhere to run.

The far-off howl of the wind was building to a wild roar as we grabbed the canteens from the saddles along with our bedrolls and hunkered down close beside the rocks. A wind chilled breeze swept over us and it was a real contrast to the heat of the day. That roan of mine was an old hand at looking out for himself in desert country. He laid down in the sand just a few feet from me, his back to the coming wind. It didn't surprise me none to see Ann crawl under the heavy tent of blankets close to Carlos while Jamie and me shared the others. The four of us were pressed up close to each other and to the rocks that were our only shelter from the storm's onslaught.

And then the storm hit.

Sand towered thousands of feet into the blazing desert sky, and that wind blew colder and colder, chilling us all to the bone. Wind blew all around us, shrieking like a banshee, and then howling like an enraged giant. The air seemed thinner, harder to breathe as the whipping winds grabbed it away and tried to smother us all. Seemed like the wind would tear up the very earth itself and toss it up into the yellowed sky. I'd been through more than one sand storm, and every time was no better'n the first. The sand worked its way through the thickest of coverings, filling a man's eyes, ears, and throat until he gagged and had to fight the urge to throw off the blankets and run out into the open. Except there was no open, only a wall of sand thick enough to cut with a knife. The wind swept away a man's sense of direction, he couldn't tell truly which was up or down, and so was left suspended in heavy, screaming air. Air that was filled with cutting, smothering sand, and that crackling feeling that made a body real fearful of what might be coming.

Seemed like forever that storm pounded at us, but when it stopped, and I stood up out of the blankets to have myself a look around, only a couple hours had passed. Ann and Carlos stood up out of a little hill of sand, straightening, and shaking the blankets free of the sand. About the same time that desert roan of mine was climbing to his feet, shaking himself and snorting. I gave him a couple of friendly pats while Jamie went to the other horses and started to untie their hobbles. The storm had been shorter than most I'd been through. In a way it'd been almost a blessing. We'd lost the Apache, that much was sure. That didn't mean we might not run across another band up ahead, but we were starting out even.

I glanced around at my three companions. 'Everybody all right?' All three of them nodded silently in answer to my question. It was like none of us wanted to break the calming silence that had settled in in the wake of the storm.

Ann rubbed both of her arms vigorously. A body could see she still felt the chill of the wind inside her. Carlos handed her a canteen, and I could see she took no more than a sip. I took me a good look at the wind-torn landscape. We'd be needing water soon. The horses couldn't go far without it. That storm would have sure enough cleaned out most of the smaller waterholes. That meant we'd have to be looking for the sheltered ones, the ones that were harder to find. I sighed. Didn't seem like nothing ever came easy.

Well there wasn't no use putting it off. We started out again, walking and leading the horses a spell to let them stretch a mite, and let us do the same. It wasn't long 'til we were back in our saddles, pointing the horses northeast. We were off course now for the Flannigan spread. To stop there we would have to double back, and it looked to me like it would be smarter to just pass it by. What was on my mind was water. Even if we'd kept on heading toward the Flannigan spread, we'd have had to find water long before reaching it. Going a different direction didn't change that none. Part of the reason I'd changed direction after the storm was because we sorely needed water. I'd heard tell of a few small mountain ranges in the general direction we were heading, and they could mean water.

The country surrounding us was wild, rocky, and except for a few rolling hills scattered around, flat. There was cactus, plenty of it, as well as mesquite and clumps of ocotillo. There was a small mountain range coming up ahead, and I figured we'd get there well before dark. If water was there, there'd be plenty of time to locate a waterhole. I'd been keeping my eyes open, watching for sign, and from what I'd seen, it was almost a sure thing that there was a

154

waterhole somewheres about. There was plenty of small animal sign, and I'd seen some birds circling.

Those mountains looked to be growing right up out of the ground like mushrooms as we come closer. It was in me to think, for the first time, that we might have a chance of reaching Tucson when Ann brought her horse up alongside mine. Carlos and Jamie stayed behind.

'There's something wrong,' Ann said pointedly. She sure was one girl who didn't mince words. 'Can't we go around those mountains?'

I shook my head. 'Figure there's water there. If we pass them, ain't no telling how long it'll be 'til we find some, if at all.'

'Ann!' Jamie exploded behind us. 'Ann! look! Those are the mountains on Pa's map! You remember! The ones he told us about back home. The ones with the flat tops like somebody cut them off with an ax. And look there.' He was pointing eagerly, 'There's where they're split with only the rock showing bare to the sun, just like he said.'

Well, that was enough to put gray in a man's hair. If those were the mountains where their pa's gold was, odds were mighty high that we'd be meeting up with somebody who wasn't too friendly to strangers about now. I'd seen gold fever more than once before. Gold was like a magnet. It drew honest miners to the country, but it also drew every saddletramp, bandito, and scum the country had to offer. Ever since the news leaked out about her pa's strike, there had been people out looking for it. It was for danged sure that Ann's uncle would be out there somewheres doing his share of looking ... and the thought came to me that Curley Bill's kin probably wouldn't be too far behind.

Right where we were, I pulled up the horses short. Everything seemed quiet enough, but that didn't mean anything. I loosened that sawed-off shotgun Turk'd given me and held it at the ready in one hand.

'You keep them out of rifle range,' I told Carlos as I jerked a thumb toward Ann and Jamie. 'I want to do some scouting before we all go waltzing on in there.'

Carlos nodded, bringing his rifle out of the saddleboot. Sitting her horse, biting her lip, Ann was looking downright worried. Most times it was hard to tell what was going on in her mind, and the not knowing could be right unsettling to a man.

Touching a heel to my roan I left the others behind as I let him move in at an easy gallop. Mindful of the fact that we were still in the heart of Apache territory, I didn't want any gunplay if there was anybody up ahead in them mountains. If somebody was up there and they were sensible kind of folks, they wouldn't want that kind of attraction for the Indians either. Trouble was, some folks just weren't sensible.

The country here was rolling, and there was plenty of mesquite around. For that much I was grateful, and kept to the shelter of the low hills as much as I could. As I drew nearer, and my eyes searched the area ahead for some sign of trouble, the hairs along the back of my neck stood up on end. Something was warning me. Most likely it was something I'd seen but hadn't made an impression on me. After so many years of wandering up and down wild country, as well as scouting for the army on occasion, there was something inside me that came alert when danger was near. My eyes had seen something that hadn't registered on my mind, and I had to find out right quick what it was. My horse picked up my nervousness, and he was walking lightfooted as I guided him around a clump of that ground hugging prickly pear. He tossed his head a couple of times. That roan of mine acted like one of them Indian war ponies when there was trouble brewing, ready to have at it.

We were coming up over a small hill, that roan and me when I saw that rifle flash again ... again? In less time than it takes to tell, I knew that was what I'd seen before, only much fainter. About the time I heard that rifle crack, I felt myself going off the back of my horse like I'd run into a too low tree branch. That ground come up and hit me pretty hard, and I missed a good sized patch of cactus by not more than a couple of inches. Whoever was doing the shooting was a fair shot, but not overly accurate. The slug hit me high in the left shoulder and it'd gone clean through without hitting any bone. Scrambling up close behind the hill I slid part way down, hoping that whoever was doing the firing wasn't high enough up to see down behind that hill. Turk's sawed-off shotgun was one thing I'd managed to hang onto, but for the moment it wasn't doing me any good. Trotting on a few more strides, that roan of mine came to a halt behind the shelter of another hilt, and he just stood there a'staring back at me. He was as surprised to see me lying back behind him as I was.

I took off my hat and set it on the barrel of that gun, slowly moving it up to where I figured that gunman's eye level to be. Another shot cracked close by, kicking up the sand, but missing my hat clean. I lowered it slow like and put the hat back on my head. At least that didn't have a hole in it. Easing back a mite, I took off my neckerchief, hastily putting it over the wound as best I could. It was bleeding some, but not enough to give me something to worry about. It hurt like hell though, and that didn't do a lot for my temper. If some folks had gold, it never occurred to them that a stranger might come on them accidentally like, and never even know they had gold. Now, I didn't know who was up there, but odds were somebody was going to get themselves killed if things kept on going like they'd started. I glanced around. Reckoned this was going to take some figuring.

CHAPTER THIRTEEN

'I got him, Bull,' Abel, he was shouting and carrying on loud enough for everyone to hear him. 'Took him right off'a his horse!'

'You didn't finish him,' Bull snapped from behind his field glasses. He wasn't given to shouting when he figured there was somebody near enough to hear. 'That boy was far from dead when he hit the sand.' Lowering the field glasses, he gave Abel an icy stare. 'Never could figure how my baby sister could'a birthed a jackass like you. You should'a let him get up closer. What do ya' think the rest of us was waiting for, boy? The first winter snows?'

Cutting a man down for no reason in particular didn't set too well with Cyrus. Seemed to him that it was the girl they were after, not the lone fella who'd been riding up on them. Even the going after the girl wasn't an idea he liked.

He took off his hat, and ran a hand through his sandy brown hair. Cyrus was the only one of the lot who had him some sense. 'Apache heard that shot, Pa,' Cyrus told his pa quietly.

That girl his pa was so set on killing was out there, and Cyrus knew she wasn't alone. There were two men and the young boy as well. Cyrus had been a'hoping they wouldn't come across her, and she'd somehow get on back East. But, she was out there. Her uncle had seen her through the field glasses. Said his nephew was out there too. That'd be the boy, he reckoned. Killing a kid was something he wasn't going to have no part of. There just wasn't no reason for it. Back in town he'd heard that the boy had been taken by the Apache, so he couldn't have had anything to do with Curley Bill getting killed. As far as the gold went, they hadn't found that mine everybody had been all fired up about anyway. Cyrus's flinty gray eyes looked more grim and hard than usual. For the first time he was thinking against his pa, and it made him nervous. It felt almost like Bull could read his thoughts, and know what was going through his mind.

'Hang the Apache!' Bull exploded. 'We got business here.' Angrily, he glanced around himself, then called Latham to him.

Jumping down from the rock from where he'd been watching below, Latham strode purposefully over to Bull. Cyrus shrugged. Things were the same as they always were. It was Latham who Pa wanted by his side. It was Latham's judgment that Pa trusted. Ever since Cyrus had been a little boy, Bull had told him he was too soft. It was only in the past couple of years that Cyrus, he'd begun to realize that he didn't care a mite what his pa thought. If he was soft, then that was the way of it, his way. There was a feeling of difference between Cyrus and his kin. He had never known any loyalty except to family, there'd never been any call to. Family loyalty was still with him, but for the first time he was a' wondering: What if they were wrong in what they were doing? The thought jarred him right down to his toes. With some trouble, he forced the thought out of his mind, and gave attention to what his pa was saying to Latham and the others.

'Somebody is gonna have to finish what this idjut nephew of mine started,' Bull snapped. His green eyes flickered over the group with him. Sharp and piercing they came to rest on Abel. Abel shuffled his feet nervously, but didn't meet Bull's steady gaze. There weren't many times Cyrus could remember when Abel could meet his pa's eyes. Usually, a cross-eyed look from Bull was enough to send Abel scurrying out of his presence.

'Looks like it's your job, Latham,' Bull growled sullenly as he tore his glance from Abel. 'Abel there ain't got the guts to finish it.'

'Sure thing, Pa.' Latham, he smiled grimly as he picked up his rifle, and started for the rocky path that led down. That there was one man right eager to pull a trigger on a wounded man.

'Pa,' Cyrus put in a mite cautiously, 'you remember what folks back in Tucson said about Matt Logan. And Abel, he didn't do much more'n wing him.'

Bull turned on his younger son. His patience was wearing thin. 'You got anything else to say, spit it out pronto, boy. I ain't got no time to waste.'

'It's just that that man's been shot, probably lost him some blood,' Cyrus told him quickly. 'It's hot out there, Pa, and I don't figure they got much water or they wouldn't a been heading here.' Cyrus shrugged. He was stalling for time, and he knew it. Why he was stalling was something he didn't rightly figure he understood himself, and it was in him to wonder if Bull figured what he was trying to do. 'What I'm saying Pa is, there ain't no reason for Latham to maybe get himself shot up when we've got us plenty of time.'

Bull was nodding in approval. 'You got some brains, boy, when you care to use 'em.' He turned to his elder son. 'Wait a spell, Latham. Let him cook some, then go on down and finish the job.'

Latham nodded, but he gave his brother a long, hard look. There was something about Cyrus that didn't set right with him.

Cyrus, he reckoned he knew what he'd said to Bull wasn't true, and it made him a mite uneasy. He knew they didn't have plenty of time, and what time they did have depended on how far away the Apache were. Apache didn't miss much, and Cyrus couldn't believe they hadn't heard that shot out there in the open desert. He didn't even know what he'd managed to accomplish, stalling that away. It wouldn't change his pa's mind none. The outcome would be the same. Cyrus was feeling cornered. This here was the worst thing he'd been tangled up in.

'Hey,' Abel shouted from where he'd been standing watch, 'lookit here!'

Bull, he stepped back up to the rocks they were using as the lookout point, and roughly shouldered Abel aside, snatching his rifle away. 'Don't just stand there gawking!' Bull snapped. 'Shoot!'

Cyrus came up behind Bull in time to see Carlos riding on into the hollow. Bull snapped him off a couple shots, but he didn't get anywhere close.

163

'I wouldn't sweat if I was you, Pa,' Latham told Bull coolly. 'Like my little brother said, it's hot down there. There's two of them now, but they ain't going nowheres.' He let his icy gaze find his brother, and Cyrus could see the laughter in his brother's cold, green eyes.

With a grunt, Bull thrust the rifle back into Abel's hands, and strode rapidly back across their makeshift camp to where Adam Tucker was looking on in silence. 'Where the hell's that gold mine?' Bull demanded of him. 'We been here two days, and I ain't seen no gold.'

Adam grimaced, and smiled coldly from the depths of his dark brown eyes. 'Don't you think I want that gold as much as you do? The map couldn't be wrong ... besides they're here, aren't they?' He was pointing toward the open desert. 'You can be sure they wouldn't be here if it wasn't for the gold.'

For the moment Bull seemed satisfied. He moved off to where Latham was standing beside Abel, cursing under his breath as he walked. Adam watched him go. Nervously, he ran a hand through his thick, black hair. He still hadn't figured a way to cut the Mortons out of the gold. To top it off, Ann and Jamie picked now to show up, and the fact that they had two men escorting them made it so he needed the Mortons again. It was true, they hadn't found the gold yet, but

164

that was only a matter of time. He stared at Bull Morton and his kin, a look of hate in his eyes. There wasn't anyone he was going to share that gold with ... not anyone at all. Adam stood up from where he'd been sitting on the ground, and automatically made an attempt at brushing the heavy dust from his clothes. As he casually walked over to see how things were going below, it was in him to wonder if there were any rewards out on the Mortons. To his way of thinking, if there were any posted, and they managed to get themselves killed, he didn't see any reason why he shouldn't be the man to collect on them. Adam shrugged. If nothing else, when he brought their bodies back to Tucson he would be a hero. The man who brought down the Mortons. The thought made him feel good. He would be rich, and famous. It might even be a nice touch to play innocent when he got back to town Make up some kind of story about the Mortons trying to jump his claim after he'd hired them to guide him out into the desert. That would sound like the Mortons ... there wouldn't be any trouble selling a story like that.

Guns had always made him nervous, but in spite of that, he'd managed to learn to use a rifle real good. Of course, he felt more sure of himself when he was the one holding the gun.

Adam moved off to the waterhole for a

drink.

'There're two of 'em down there now,' Bull was telling Latham, 'you best take Abel on down there with you.'

Adam dipped his cupped hand into the water and raised it to his lips. He wasn't a man to smile very often, but he was smiling now.

CHAPTER FOURTEEN

Being holed up in that hollow behind that hill, alone, and hugging the ground, was making me feel a mite uncomfortable, but it wasn't nothing compared to what I felt when I first laid eyes on Carlos making his way in my direction. That boy had him a lot of sand or he was plumb loco. I glanced back in the direction he was coming from. There wasn't hide nor hair of Ann or Jamie to be seen. But then again, I was staying mighty close to the ground, and there wasn't nothing much that I really could see. Carlos must have put Ann and Jamie somewhere where he figured they'd be safe from that bunch up ahead. Trouble was, they weren't our only worry. A couple of shots had been fired, and them Apache weren't never far from my mind.

Carlos came riding in at a gallop, dropped from his horse's back only a few feet from me

166

and scrambled through the sand to my side. That horse of his kept on going until he caught up with my roan, and was content to stop there.

'Must be four or five of them up there,' Carlos said as he came up to me. 'We could see them clearer farther back.'

I nodded shortly. 'Figured there had to be more than one.' I sat up a little straighter. 'Where're Ann and Jamie?'

Carlos grinned. 'I told Jamie to take care of his sister, and we'd signal when it was all right for them to come in. The next time I turned around they were gone. That Jamie moves like an Indian.'

At least they were out of rifle range. I figured them both to have enough sense to know to keep clear of the shooting. Leastways, that's what I was counting on.

'You absorb lead well, my friend,' Carlos said dryly as he glanced at my shoulder wound.

'Somebody's aim was off,' I answered, 'or if we're lucky, maybe their sights are bent.'

Carlos gave me a sideways grin. 'Do you have any idea what it is we're going to do now?'

Looking toward Carlos, I shrugged. 'Don't seem like we should stay here does it? I was fixing to light a shuck when you came up.' I hefted my gun and glanced in the direction of the horses. It didn't seem too

167

far, and the hills would give us good cover. I started to stand up.

'Oh, oh,' Carlos said softly. 'Looks like we have company.'

Leaning back against the slope in the ground, I followed his gaze up the nearby slope. Two men were making their way down what appeared to be a mighty narrow trail. We couldn't really get a good look at the pair because they kept bobbing up and down amongst the rocks and brush. One thing was for sure, they weren't coming peaceful.

Now I don't like trouble, never have. Mostly, I steer clear of it when I can. Trouble was, I had a powerful mean temper when trouble was dumped on my door. And here those two were bringing it to me. When men come after me with rifles, I don't see no reason for pulling in my horns.

'I count two,' I told him. 'That what you've got?'

Carlos breathed his reply. 'I think that is all.' His deep black eyes were solemn as he wiped the sweat from his forehead beneath the brim of his hat, and kept his rifle at the ready.

'I'm going to circle off to the side, and see if I can hit 'em broadside,' I said to Carlos. 'Keep the others off my back. If you see them coming down off that trail, you best do something about it.'

He grinned and checked the load in his rifle. When a man does that, a body knows he's done his share of fighting. He knows the value of knowing how many shots he's packing, and being sure he has a full load. It sure enough doesn't pay to have your gun click down on an empty chamber when you're looking down another man's gun-barrel.

Packing that shotgun of Turk's I knew I had only four shots, but that thing was like a cannon. It was plumb hard to miss. 'Sides, there was always my handgun. That was carrying a full load. Skirting around the bottom edge of the hill where I'd been holed up, I worked my way toward the steep slope of the mountain. As mountains went, these were downright small, but the slope was still steep enough to really make me sweat when I started working my way up. I hadn't drawn any lead from above, so either they hadn't seen me, or they were figuring on letting me get closer before they tried to finish me off. Thing they didn't know was that I wasn't fixing to get myself too close to them up on the mountainside. The men coming down toward me were the ones I was after.

There was a lot of black chaparral thereabouts, thick and thorny. Most times it was no friend to me, being good for nothing 'sides tearing up good clothes and scratching up good horses. For a time though, things were different. It was thick enough to give some good cover. Sidestepping clumps of cholla and prickly pear as I went, I slipped from one clump to another.

Laying up close to a couple good-sized rocks and some chaparral, I spotted the pair of men coming down off that trail Carlos had seen earlier. They hadn't spotted me yet, and so I just lay quiet, my gun cocked and ready. Some gunshots cut loose above me, but the slugs weren't giving me anything to go worrying about. I drew myself up as small as I could behind them rocks and got up to where I was sitting on my heels, gun ready ... waiting. It wasn't in me to go looking to kill anybody, but I never had been one to sit and wait while it was brought to me. When trouble showed, it was best for a man to meet it on his own chosen ground.

Them two kept on a'coming, and there wan't no doubt of it, they had their guns out. I couldn't rightly recognize them, through the chaparral and all, but the way the smaller one moved reminded me of someone that I couldn't place, and that voice I heard before had me figuring that bunch for Mortons. I waited a few more seconds, leading them with that cannon of Turk's, keeping them in my sights.

They weren't more'n fifteen yards from me when I stood up. The way I was standing in that brush there wasn't much of me they

170

could see except my head, shoulders, and that gun.

'That's about far enough,' I said flatly. 'You boys drop your guns before somebody gets hurt.'

Well, they turned toward me, and I knew then why that smaller one looked familiar. That there was Abel Jenkins, that would'a been his voice shouting out a spell earlier too, and the one with him could only be another one of Curley Bill Morton's kin. I figured for sure the rest of them up above had to be the same. I'd a had me something to ponder on, taking Abel Jenkins and one of Curley Bill's kin prisoner out there. That is, if I'd a had the time. There he was, a'looking down twin barrels of a cannon, me not needing to aim at all, and that damn fool tried to get the drop on me. That gun of his was coming up mighty fast, and I just plain didn't have no choice. I pulled the trigger. That gun exploded in my hands, the shot jarring me like I'd been mule kicked, and that long-faced, tall-bodied boy took almost the whole charge full in the chest. It threw him back, half turning him around as he fell into one of the ground-crawling patches of prickly pear. Didn't matter to him though, he was dead before he hit the ground. The sound of that single shot rolled off into the hills like a herd of stampeding horses.

Abel, he'd been standing a mite too close.

He was laying there on the ground where he fell, a'moaning and cussing. His gun was still in his holster and he wasn't making any move to get it. I relaxed some, but kept that gun aimed at him.

'You didn't have to go and do that,' Abel whined, 'I wasn't pulling no gun.'

I shrugged. 'It's the company you keep.' Looked to me like his left side was pretty well peppered, but it didn't look to be fatal. I scratched my chin and gave him a cool look. 'Tell you what ... the way I figure it, you got kin up there, so you climb on back up there to them. Tell them all we want is water.'

Them sneaky brown eyes of his widened, and he gasped. 'Hell mister, I can't make it back up there.'

'Sure you can,' I told him reassuringly. 'Be surprised what you can do if you put your mind to it.' I took the gun from his holster, then went and fetched the one from the fool who tried to draw on a shotgun, and moseyed on down the side of the slope. Abel, he was still laying there when I left, but he was no worry of mine.

'You're a dead man, mister,' Abel called after me all of a sudden. 'That there was Bull Morton's son you laid out.'

He could have just as well been talking to the wind, for I wasn't paying him any mind. There were other things that needed figuring. Those others were still up above,

172

holding the waterhole we needed. I'd a just reloaded that gun I was packing to a full four shells and gone up there to take my chances. Trouble was, I wasn't alone. Ann, Jamie, and Carlos needed that water too. If I went and got myself killed, it'd make it that much harder for them to get it.

'I heard the shots,' Carlos told me as I slid down beside him, 'along with every Apache within twenty miles. What happened?'

'Nailed one, clipped another's wings,' I said as I filled the gun's empty chamber. 'They ain't inviting company up, so we're going to have to get that water our own way.'

CHAPTER FIFTEEN

'What about Latham?' Bull snapped viciously at Abel.

Cyrus, he'd gone part way down the trail after that last shot rolled across the hills. They were figuring it for a shotgun. He'd come back hauling Abel with him.

'He's dead, Bull,' Abel whined. He was afraid to tell his uncle what'd happened. 'That fella Logan cut him down with some fancy gun. I tried to help Latham,' he lied, 'but he caught me too. It was only 'cause he figured I'd never make it back that he didn't finish me right there.' Abel, he was a right quick thinking, quick lying man. Me, figuring he'd find a way a'lookin' out for himself was sure enough right.

'Dead?' Bull nearly shouted the word, but he looked pained and glared at the other men around him. 'Dead!' Bull's anger was reaching a new peak. 'I'll tear that ranny apart with my bare hands.'

Cyrus stood back a couple of paces, surprised with himself at how little his older brother's death meant to him. He and Latham had never been what you might call close, but he'd been his brother, and family ties had always been strong. It wasn't in him to feel a great urge for revenge as his father did. Cyrus watched Bull. He knew him, knew how to figure him better'n most. Now Bull's rage was directed at those below, but when it was all over, Bull would still be mourning for Latham, and then nothing short of a miracle would keep Abel alive. Cyrus knew how his father's mind worked, but at the same time didn't want to admit it to himself.

Out of habit, Cyrus picked up the field glasses, and gazed out across the open desert that spread out in all four directions. Far off to the southwest he could see a cloud of dust rising. He knew the country, and he knew what that dust meant.

'Pa,' Cyrus called urgently. 'Pa, you better take a look at this.'

Striding across the clearing, Bull grabbed the field glasses from his son. 'Well?' he bellowed.

'Apache, Pa,' Cyrus explained, 'and I reckon there's a passel of them.'

'So? We fit Indians before,' Bull said sharply, 'we got business here.'

'Not this time, Pa,' Cyrus urged. 'We'd better clear out while we can. There must be twenty-five, maybe thirty of them, and only me and you to fight 'em. Abel, he's all shot up, and that Adam Tucker, he ain't no use.' Cyrus, he was talking faster in his excitement. 'Pa,' he went on, 'if we clear out now, maybe the Apache'll finish them off. And even if they don't finish them, they'll have to come to Tucson. We can be waiting for them there.'

Bull spun around, shaking his son's hand from his arm, and glared around him, his green eyes flashing a white hot hate. Abel was still sprawled right where Cyrus had left him, and that Tucker fella was standing over by the waterhole.

He stared hard at Cyrus. 'You're all I got left, boy. We'll do it your way, leastways this time we will.' Bull ran a hand through his hair as he threw a glance in Adam's direction. 'Mount up,' he ordered, 'we're clearing out.'

Adam looked real unhappy at the words, but before he could say anything to Bull, the big man brushed right on past to stand over his nephew.

'You best climb up on your horse, boy,' Bull stated flatly, 'or we'll leave you right where you lay.'

Abel groaned and clutched his arm some tighter up against his injured side. His uncle wasn't playing games. There weren't many folks who figured Bull Morton would do anything besides exactly what he said he would. Abel, he knew it too. Groaning again, he rolled to his knees, then staggered unsteadily to his feet. Cyrus had said something about Apache, he'd heard that clear enough. If them Indians caught him here alone, he didn't need to be told what would happen. Limping and shuffling over to his horse, Abel dragged himself up into the saddle. Bull didn't even look back to see if Abel had done what he was told. He just swung his horse up alongside his only son's and they lit out for other parts. His nephew, Abel Jenkins, and that greenhorn Adam Tucker were right behind them, but as far as Bull was concerned, they were on their own.

The Apache were still a good ways off from the mountains when Bull Morton and the rest of them with him pulled out. They were a'throwing up quite a dust cloud in their leaving, and them Indians knew the difference between a dust devil and some horses moving out mighty fast. When they saw that dust cloud moving off to the northeast, they did the natural thing ... they swung more north, cutting cross-country to try and catch them.

CHAPTER SIXTEEN

Carlos and me split up and started working our way toward where we figured them fellas to be holed up. The waterhole would have to be there. It wasn't 'til we were nearly halfway up that I noticed there wasn't no lead flying in our direction. I stopped a second and waited. There wasn't anything moving around up above, leastways nothing I could hear. Reckon it could'a been a trap, but I doubted it. Still, it didn't pay to go taking chances, so I stayed low and kept moving. The sun was burning through my clothes, and the heat rising off'a the ground felt like it was coming off a campfire. Sweat had broke out across my forehead, and my sleeve was stiff with my own blood dried up against the flesh wound I'd picked up when I rode in.

After what seemed like a whole lot of years, I reached the top of the trail where it opened up into a kind of flat plateau circled by rocks, brush, and cactus. My gun drawn, I slipped forward as Carlos came up over the other side. There was an empty feeling about the place. I shook my head and glanced toward Carlos who shrugged and did the same. It sure beat all how folks thought. First, they shoot at me like some wild bear at bay, and managed to lose one of their own while they were doing it, then they just pull out like nothing happened. It gave me a good case of the worries. That Abel Jenkins ran with the Morton crowd. He was some kin of theirs, and he'd said I killed Bull Morton's son. Well, that was a fact, he was still lying back yonder on the trail. It gave me reason to wonder what the hell was going on. I knew better than to think this thing had run out its string. Bull Morton wasn't a man to cut and run for no reason, and he wasn't a man to forget either.

'You had better have a look here, amigo,' Carlos said from behind me. 'There is the reason our friends left so quickly.'

Off a ways to the southwest of us I could make out a good sized dust cloud. That meant there was a whole passel of riders, and out here that meant Apache. A little north of us and heading northeast was a smaller dust cloud, and it was still close enough to make out the small shapes of bobbing riders though it was moving away fast. Somebody with them had some sense, clearing out thataway. Looked to me like they had a big enough lead to slip clear. That was, if one of them had some trail sense.

Pondering some on them dust clouds, I caught sight of some movement out of the corner of my eye and swung full around, my gun at the ready.

'Ann, Jamie,' Carlos called out to them cheerfully, relief plain in his voice. He went straight over to Ann to help her down.

Me, I put down my gun and looked up at them while Jamie climbed down. They even had our horses with them.

'Jamie kept us pretty far out in the chaparral,' Ann informed us quietly as she slipped to the ground in Carlos's arms. 'But we saw those fellows up there leave, and Jamie spotted Indians heading this way, so we decided we'd better take a chance and come on up.' Ann slipped out of Carlos's encircling arms, but it looked to me like she'd a liked to have kept them where they were.

'It was a chance all right,' I told her, 'but you did right.'

I glanced back toward the two dust clouds below us. The larger was changing its direction, cutting across toward the smaller. Well, that suited me just fine. That Morton bunch was drawing them Indians off 'a us. They wouldn't be figuring some folks stayed behind in the mountains.

'Water the horses and keep them quiet,' I said quickly. 'We don't want anything changing their minds for them, and bringing them over this way. We'll stay here a spell and rest the horses.'

Carlos wandered back from the waterhole to rejoin us, and I noticed something dangling from his hand.

'Found this over by the water.' He turned it around in his hand a couple of times. 'It looks like some kind of pouch.' He started to open it, and it opened flat in his hand. The leather was marked by a series of lines and arrows.

'That was my father's map,' Ann was very excited. 'But how?' she began, then cut herself short as she took the map out of Carlos's hand. 'My uncle was here ... he was with them.' The disgust in her voice was plain enough. Her wide brown eyes held mine in their steady gaze. 'He's after the gold. That means he still wants to kill me,' she finished softly, as she fingered the small piece of leather.

I nodded slowly. 'Likely,' I told her. 'But he ain't about to get the chance to try right now. They lit out. And that was Morton's crowd he was with. I just managed to cut down another one of his sons. Don't reckon he'll be looking too kindly on that, so I figure us to be in this together about as tight as two turtles in one shell.'

Looking puzzled, Carlos frowned. 'In what?' he asked, 'I don't understand all this.'

Jamie was over by the horses, out of earshot. 'She killed Curley Bill Morton and a friend of his, Jed Sloan, in self-defense.' I was glad Jamie wasn't close enough to hear me tell Carlos what had happened.

His dark eyes widened and Carlos looked questioningly at Ann. 'You querida? But how?'

Ann looked a little nervous as she brushed a few stray strands of her auburn hair back from her face, but she gave Carlos a quick, no nonsense version of how things went before he joined up with us at his father's ranchero.

'You have bad trouble,' Carlos said when Ann had finished as he let his soft black eyes move back and forth between us. 'The Mortons are known even in Mexico.' He looked at Ann real serious. 'They will not harm you while I live,' he said quietly. Then he cheered up a mite and gave me a lop-sided grin. 'But, if it is as you said, there should be only two of them waiting for us in Tucson.'

Grinning back at him I took off my battered old trail hat to knock some of the dust off. 'That family multiplies faster'n a pack of rats,' I told him. 'They got kin scattered all over this territory, and you can bet they let them know there was trouble before they ever left Tucson. What's going to be waiting for us there ain't too hard to figure, and you can be danged sure I'm going in loaded for bear.'

A little startled by what I'd said, Ann looked hard at me. For a moment, it seemed like she was reading the lines on my face, using them like a map to see that was going on inside my head. Seemed like people never did what other folks expected of them.

I shrugged. There was no way of telling what was going on in her mind, and right then it was no concern to me. What did concern me was getting myself a drink and making sure the horses were tended to. The sun was already beginning to swing low in the western sky, lighting up the distant horizon with a golden glow. We'd camp here the night, make do without a fire, then start out for Tucson with the first light. We were still some better than a couple days out of Tucson. Looked to me like we were going to make it which seemed to be more a surprise to me than anybody else. It wasn't in me to be a cautious man, but it seemed to me that now would be the wrong time to let our guard down. Carlos and I would have to split the watch. If them Apache came back the same way they went, they'd likely be stopping off where we were for water, and I wasn't of a mind to get trapped up on the mountain. There were stories about folks getting themselves killed right outside of town. How close you were to town didn't matter much in this country, unless a body could run almighty fast.

As planned, we spent the first night there on that mountain. The moon was bright, near full, the air was cool and refreshing like a mountain stream. Our luck held ... them Apache didn't come back our way. Carlos had the first watch, and I stood second watch until near dawn. When we broke camp and saddled up in the gray light of early morning there wasn't nobody a'dawdling. Jamie, he'd learned a lot from them Indians. He didn't go wasting any time when he got to work. Ann, she was sticking mighty close to Carlos.

The horses had been watered and rested so we pushed hard all that day, running into no trouble. We spotted a couple of bands of Apache, but I reckon they weren't figuring on anybody else being around except themselves. The way it worked out, we slipped past them and saved everybody a big ruckus. Come sundown, we made a dry camp, and no fire. Only thing out in the chaparral that night was an owl and a few coyotes hunting up something to eat. A couple of smokes west of us were spotted just as we dug in for the night. They weren't concerning us, so I just put them from my mind.

The moon, full and bright, was still hanging low in the sky when the sun came up the next morning. The day started hot and stayed that way, but I was real determined that we wouldn't spend another night in camp in Apache country. Quite a ways back we had crossed back into the land of the giant saguaro cactus, and now the mesquite was thick. We rode wary, half expecting a band of Apache to come sweeping down some dry wash at us at any time. My rifle was out across my saddle at the ready. Carlos's gun was right handy too, and all of us rode with feet light in the stirrups.

That night we made Tucson, though it was late, and it didn't look like much more than a dark blotch on the land. There were a couple lights showing feebly from far spread windows, one of them being the saloon. Alone, I would have ridden in with little thought as to what might be waiting. I wasn't given to worrying about things that *might* happen and never did. Trouble was, this time I was mindful of having Ann and Jamie with me. As for Carlos, well he saddled his own bronc. He could handle himself, and it sure looked to me like he was watching out for Ann as well, though I didn't let up because of it. Just outside of town I paused a bit, giving a few minutes to pondering what would be on the mind of Bull Morton, providing he'd made it back to town. Of the latter, I had little doubt. Didn't figure we could be lucky enough to have had him killed out in the desert somewhere by the

Apache or even just an ornery sidewinder.

I looked around real careful like a couple of times. The streets were empty, but that didn't mean there weren't no prying eyes about. There wasn't much to see from where we were setting, even though the darkness had never made much difference to me. But even a man with the best of eyes for darkness couldn't see through buildings.

Seemed to me like it'd be best if we kept to the shadows and maybe kept folks guessing for a spell. I led off toward the back street that ran behind Turk's saloon. Just naturally seemed like the best place to lay low ... for tonight anyhow. And ol' Turk, he could probably hide Ann and Jamie longer than that if he was pressed to. By now I figured I owed Turk a little pressing.

Turk didn't have the back door latched, so I slipped on inside the back room leading the way for the others. The door was eased shut behind us by Carlos, then he slipped up alongside me to have a look at the bar. The hour was getting late, but still I counted eleven men out there. Four were playing cards at one of the tables in the corner, two more were doing some serious drinking near the door, and the others were scattered out along the bar. I spotted Turk right off, tending bar as usual. It looked to me like we were going to have some waiting to do. Most likely, Turk would come to the back room every once in a while, but it could be some time before he had a reason to. Easing the door closed, I cut off the shaft of light that had been slicing through the darkness. Even so, some light managed to filter through the not so tightly fitted boards, and under the door. Turk's back room was cluttered with kegs, empty and full, a couple of crates of spare glasses not yet needed, and some full sacks of grain like maybe Turk was figuring on brewing some of his own. There were a lot of empty bottles laying in a corner. It would be like Turk to figure on a little larger profit by making some brew of his own. He wasn't a man who missed out much on opportunity. If I recalled right, he had himself a still back in that New Orleans bar too.

I found myself a keg and sat down. 'Looks like we'll have to wait a spell,' I told them in a low tone. 'Stretch out on some of them old sacks and catch some shut-eye,' I advised Ann and Jamie.

Carlos leaned silently against a wall and remained on his feet. 'You think there will be trouble, amigo?' he asked as he leaned his rifle against the wall.

'Don't rightly know,' I shrugged, 'but I reckon that's what I'm figuring on. Turk's a man who knows his town,' I told Carlos, 'if there's something in the wind hereabouts he'll be the first to sniff it, especially if it's trouble.' I let my rifle butt rest between my feet, the barrel pointing toward the roof.

The door to the saloon opened abruptly and Turk's tall, wiry figure stood framed in the light spilling through the doorway a few seconds before he stepped inside. The harsh light fell along the planes of his face making it look even harder and more grim than usual.

'Close the door,' I breathed urgently into the semidarkness while I kept clear of that spot of light so's nobody out there by the bar could get a good look at me. His black hair glistened in the false light and I could almost feel them cool, gray eyes of his swing around in my direction.

A deep chuckle rumbled deep in the throat of Turk as he swung the door closed, and strode across the board floor to lock me in one of his bear hugs. 'I was plumb worried out, boy.' His voice was a rumbling whisper. He released his bone-mashing grip as he took a step back. I could almost feel his smile in the room when he caught sight of Ann and Jamie. Then his gaze fell on Carlos. 'Who's he?' Turk threw the question in my direction. He wasn't much for standing on ceremony.

'Carlos Otero,' Carlos put in before I could answer.

Turk nodded his appreciation. 'From that big spread south of the border, I've heard of it.' His curiosity satisfied, Turk turned his attention back to me. 'You did right, boy, coming the back way like you did. Near the whole Morton clan is buzzing around Tucson like flies to dead meat. The word is they're waiting for you to show yourself. Old Bull Morton knows who you are and he's letting folks around here know that anybody who helps you isn't any friend of his.' Turk looked a mite unhappy. 'What the hell did you do to him, boy? He doesn't have any love for the little lady here either,' Turk gestured in Ann's direction. Scratching his chin he went on quickly. 'You stay here. I have to get back out there or they'll start to think I'm up to something. A couple of them are Morton's men. It'll be a few hours yet before I close down for the night. Make yourselves comfortable,' he added with a broad gesture, then left us alone again in the dim light of his back room.

I glanced over at Carlos and shrugged. All we could do was wait.

CHAPTER SEVENTEEN

Bull Morton was roaring drunk which wasn't no surprise to anyone, and in a town the size of Tucson folks could hear that bellering, even behind locked shutters. It happened regular, whenever he hit a town big enough to supply whiskey for his large thirst, which was most of them. He'd followed his pattern for three nights. His six-foot-four-inch frame folded into a spindly chair beside a window, a bottle in one hand and his glass in the other. The streets below their hotel window were still and dark, but he stared down on them a'waiting for me to show myself.

Doing nothing but sleep ever since the doc got finished with him, Abel Jenkins was a'laying quietly on the bed. The doc didn't figure him to be leaving this world real soon if infection didn't set in. He hadn't been interested in much of anything since he'd taken part of that load that'd killed Latham. That Abel had made it back to town carrying that buckshot in his side hadn't surprised Cyrus none. He figured he knew it hadn't been a matter of courage, for Abel it had been more like a study in cowardice. It had been fear that'd brought him through, fear of what those Apache would have done to him if Bull had left him behind. Cyrus, he sat in a straight-backed chair near the door, leaning forward, his head in his hands. His shaggy, sandy-colored hair was hanging forward, worked through with grit, sand and sweat.

Those Apache had come close, damn close to running them down, and Cyrus alone of all of them had really known how close they'd come. Abel had been too tore up to notice anything, Bull was too single-minded, and that Eastern fella, Tucker, wouldn't have enough sense to be scared if an Apache was standing over him with a scalping knife. Seemed like all he could do was to keep demanding that they go on back and find that gold. Cyrus glanced over to where Adam Tucker sat in one of them big, overstuffed, wing-back chairs that occupied the corner of the room beside the bed where Abel lay. Adam bothered Cyrus. Just being in the same room with Adam was enough to foul the air as far as Cyrus was concerned. He would just as soon be rid of him, but Bull wanted him around for some reason, so he stayed.

Cyrus let his flinty gaze slip past Abel and Adam over to where his pa was slumped in his chair, the empty bottle dangling from near limp fingers. Cyrus had taken a couple of drinks himself, but he figured somebody had to be sober if something came up. His pa was taking losing Latham pretty hard. Latham's death didn't bother Cyrus none, and it surprised him that he wasn't more affected by his brother's death than he was.

He stroked his thick, bushy mustache and looked over toward Adam. After a moment, Cyrus dropped his eyes, rubbing them a bit, giving thought to what he knew would soon happen. Bull'd rounded up every cousin, friend, and man who owed the Mortons a favor. Bull Morton had what amounted to a small army right here in Tucson, and it was all for one man. Cyrus sighed and tried to steel himself to the killing that he knew would be coming real soon.

Adam glanced up, his cold, brown eyes raking Cyrus with a malignant stare. He wasn't a patient or forgiving man, and about now he was getting mighty concerned about that gold. They'd been so close to it, and Bull had let Cyrus talk him into clearing out because of the Apache. They could have stayed. They could have stood those Indians off if Bull had given it half a chance. Now, since they returned to town he hadn't been out of the sight of some Morton or friend of theirs hardly long enough to answer the call of nature, let alone do anything about his own affairs. They had him penned good, at least for the moment. Adam knew what they were trying to do. They still wanted their share of the gold, and had no notion of letting him slip off by himself. Coldly, he wished them all dead. They were all complications, and Adam figured the whole thing had gotten out of hand.

Ann and the others with her stopped at that waterhole on the mountain. Had she found the gold? It was possible. If she had, Adam figured he'd give his eye teeth to get a hold of her. If she hadn't gotten the gold, then, getting her would be a lot of trouble for nothing. Taking out one of the thin cigars he sometimes smoked, Adam let his cold gaze slide around the small hotel room.

That Cyrus. It would have been a lot easier if he was more like his father, and had drunk himself into a dead sleep. He'd made himself a burr under Adam's saddle for days. He lit the cigar and drew the smoke deep into his lungs. Whatever he finally tried, he would have to be careful. He'd picked him up enough to know it was dangerous to cross the Mortons.

Adam smiled to himself as he reached into his pocket where he'd stuffed that leather map. He had had no reason for looking at it since they'd been back at that waterhole, but now he wanted the feel of it in his hands. He reached into his pocket, and the feel of leather didn't brush up against his fingertips. Adam frowned and tried again, pulling both pockets inside out in his desperate search. He was shaken to the soles of his boots. The map was gone. Frantic, he looked around the room, but there was no one looking in his direction to see his panic ... at least no one he noticed. Could he find the place again without the map. Out there, in all that sandy emptiness? He didn't like to think about it, but he knew he would have to try soon.

From beneath partially lowered lids Adam kept an eye on Cyrus as Cyrus walked to a window to have him a look-see at the dark street below. The plain self-confidence of Bull's son ate at him. Cyrus wouldn't have any trouble finding the single spot out in the middle of the desert where they'd just come from. Adam ground his teeth, near biting his cigar in half.

Cyrus would never turn on his pa, that much Adam knew about him. But what if his father was dead, then there'd be no reason for him to refuse to take Adam back to the gold. Adam's face was grim and set. It was something to think about. If Cyrus ever found out Adam was in some way responsible for the death of his pa, he'd be apt to turn on him like one of them half-tamed circus cats.

The first bright glare of the morning sun caught the corner window of their room as Bull stirred in his chair and showed the first signs of returning to the world of the living. He loosened fingers that had grown stiff during the night from holding the neck of the empty bottle, and let it drop to the wooden floor with a hollow thud. He muttered something that couldn't be understood, and climbed to his feet snarling and rubbing his beefy hands vigorously over his face. He swayed on his feet some, looking like some giant, ready to topple from his own weight. With feet far spread, he managed to keep his balance, and cursed at the pain in his head, all the while scratching himself real thorough like. Staring around a few seconds like a bear just coming out of hibernation, he spotted his son sitting in the window frame, looking down on the street.

'Anything stirring, Cyrus?' Bull asked, through what felt like a mouth full of cotton.

Cyrus shrugged. 'Nothing that I can see, Pa. Just some town's folks goin' about their business.'

Bull leaned across his son, and gulped in the still, cool morning air. After a moment, he grunted and turned back into the room. Adam's eyes never left him from where he sat near Abel's bed.

'Get out of here,' Bull roared in Adam's direction.

Adam was near blasted out of his chair. Without a word to the big man, Adam turned deliberately on his heel and left the hotel room, his bootheels ringing on the floorboards as he went. Cyrus had half turned from the window, and stared at his father in puzzlement. Bull's outburst caught them by surprise. It'd been Bull who wanted to keep Adam around.

'Just decided I don't like him,' Bull snapped. 'Hell, you can find where that gold is supposed to be hid without him. And the man ain't got no backbone. Wouldn't be a lick of help when the shooting starts. Never can trust a man who'll turn on his own kin.' Bull dropped into the overstuffed wing chair

Adam had just left. Scratching his chin through his wiry black beard he glanced at his son. 'Let's go on down and rustle us some of that good grub they serve here for breakfast.'

Cyrus swung into the room, checked his gun, and followed his pa out the door. He'd seen Adam come out of the hotel door below. He had him a gut feeling about that Tucker fella, and it wasn't good. If he'd'a known how far Adam Tucker would go, Cyrus would'a known that was trouble he'd seen walking out that door.

CHAPTER EIGHTEEN

It was well on to morning before Turk finally closed up and came to fetch Carlos and me from that back room. Jamie and Ann were both sleeping so we just let them lay. Turk's place was closed up as usual at the end of a long night, shades pulled and door locked.

Carlos and me were both trail weary and covered with grit that felt like it'd become a part of our skin. Dust clung to everything, and when a man sweated it turned to mud. I had me a pretty good beard started, being on the trail so many days. Carlos's jaw was thick with black stubble, him not being with us from the outset. It felt good to sit down somewhere that wasn't on a horse's back, and not have to twist my neck to see around behind and every which way at the same time. Nine days out on that desert, sharing it with them Apache, did a lot to take the starch out of a man.

'Had a good friend, with a very closed mouth, take care of your horses,' Turk said as he gestured for us to take one of the far corner tables deep in the shadows.

I brought up the shotgun Turk'd loaned me for the trip and laid it across the table. 'It came in right handy a couple times,' I told him quietly, 'it's a good friend to have.'

Managing to include Carlos in his gaze, Turk glanced at the gun, then back to me. 'You really bought it this time, boy,' he told me. 'I don't think you better trust anybody in this town. Half of them are Morton's men, and the other half just townfolk who're scared stiff.'

Carlos blinked. 'What about the one who you said took our horses to care for them? And the law?'

'Oh him, he's just a kid.' Turk brought a pitcher of beer and some glasses, and sat down with us. 'He'll keep his mouth shut, but I don't want him around during any shooting.' Turk shrugged. 'As for the law'—he spread his hands—'it comes and goes. Mostly, it goes.'

I nodded. 'That's about what I was

figuring.' I paused. 'We're going to have to keep Ann and Jamie out of sight if Bull Morton decides he wants a war.'

Turk's gray eyes were sharp, glinting in the dim half light of the coming dawn. 'That's exactly what he wants, from what I can see. He's got men spread all over Tucson, and they're all watching for you to show yourself.' He gave a sideways grin. 'There is a small cellar under some floorboards out back. Ann and Jamie can hide there. No one knows about it but me.'

I shrugged. It was better than nothing. 'You reckon there's any chance of us slipping out and making tracks once it gets dark?' I poured myself a tall beer from that pitcher and looked intently at Turk, waiting for an answer.

Turk shrugged his broad shoulders. 'Anything's possible,' he said doubtfully, 'but you have to remember, if you don't make it, all of you will be looking down a lot of gunbarrels.'

'Figured that's what you'd say.' I took a long pull on my beer. 'Looks like we stand and fight,' I said simply.

Carlos nodded. 'It is better for us to surprise them, than for them to surprise us.'

'You've got yourself a good head,' Turk said to Carlos. 'They don't know you're in town yet, so you should be able to do some damage before they can figure out what hit them.'

'Reckon we'd better lay low today,' I told Turk. 'Tonight when you open up you can duck your head in the back room when some of Morton's men show up. We'll give those boys a little surprise, and then figure where to go from there.'

We finished that pitcher of beer between us, then Carlos and me went back into Turk's back room to find us a couple of cots. Some shut-eye was what we were needing then most. I knew Turk would be standing watch with that small cannon of his, so I just naturally relaxed for the first time in days. It felt good, stretching out on that cot and closing my eyes, knowing I didn't have to worry none about whether I was ever going to open them again.

Seemed like I hadn't more than closed my eyes when Ann brought me awake with a touch. All at once I came awake figuring there was trouble, but Ann just smiled and handed me a plate of some kind of stew. When I glanced around, I saw it was late afternoon, and from the saloon beyond the door I could hear the low talk of early customers. Carlos was standing over by the door, eating his stew and peering through a knothole at the same time. The smell of the food drifted up from the plate I held and I realized how hungry I was.

'A boy brought it around the back way. He

said Turk sent it,' Ann said softly. It was plain to see she was real cautious about who might be able to hear her words.

I just nodded and started putting the food where it belonged, in my stomach. Glancing around as I ate, I spotted Jamie watching the back way through a hole in a curtain covering the only window in the back of the building. Few people passed that way and there was no light in the back room to give us away. Still, it was best to stand a watch. A man did well to know when trouble was coming. The vittles finished, I set my plate aside, moving quietly to where Carlos was standing by the door.

Carlos motioned for me to look through the knothole. 'Whenever someone comes in that Turk thinks I should have a look at, he puts his towel on top of the bar,' he told me in a whisper. 'Otherwise, he leaves it underneath.'

I grinned. Turk would have made a good spy a few years back during the war between the states. I put my eye up against that knothole and was surprised at how much I could see. There were only three men in the saloon. Probably some of the townspeople slipping in early for a drink or two before the big boys showed up for the night of drinking, gambling, and general roughhousing. I moved away from the hole in the door and straightened up. There was nothing we could

199

do 'til dark, and that was still a couple of hours away. Even then, it would be better for us to wait until most of the Morton bunch had a few drinks under their belts before we made any move. We were fixing to take on a mighty big mouthful to chew, and I was hoping we wouldn't choke.

Nightfall came with a suddenness that plunged the little back room into darkness as if a lantern had been snuffed out. The only light was what snaked in under the heavy wooden door, and some that came through the knothole where Carlos was still standing watch. He motioned to me silently in the dim, gray light. Ann sat quietly watching us as I slipped up to the door to join him. Jamie was still watching the back way though I had my doubts as to what he might be able to see. It was black as pitch out behind the saloon. The noise out front was growing noticeably louder as more men drifted in.

'The one on the far end of the bar,' Carlos said as I slipped up beside him.

I looked out into the well-lighted saloon, and let my gaze wander down the bar to the far end. A tall man leaned up against the bar nursing the drink Turk'd just poured out in front of him. He was thin as a rail, and looked to be tough as old leather as he lounged there apart from the others in the saloon. There was a wolfish look about his face. I'd never seen the man before, but it wasn't any trick to recognize a gunny when I saw one.

'There're two more over at the corner table,' Carlos redirected my attention.

My eyes had just started a circuit of the room when Carlos pinpointed the pair I'd run across. They were a mangy looking pair, rough as old tree bark and poison mean. Starting trouble wasn't something I liked doing, but it seemed to me that trouble was waiting long before we hit town. They were hunting it, and nothing would give me more pleasure than to clip their horns. I glanced at Carlos, and hefted my rifle to check the load, then did the same for the gun that hung at my hip. I could almost feel Ann's eyes on me in the room's dim light.

Ann came up beside me, her eyes fastened on the gun I was handling. 'Can't we get on our horses and go somewhere else? Further north maybe? It's dark, we could slip past them.' Jamie turned from his place at the window, and I could almost see the glint in his round, brown eyes from where I stood. Even Jamie knew better than that.

''Fraid not,' I told her. 'Lady luck was sitting on our shoulders the first time, but I doubt we'd be that lucky twice.'

Rubbing both her arms with her hands like she was cold, even though it was plenty warm in there, Ann glanced away from me. Carlos came up and said something to her

that I couldn't hear and I saw her nod. It
didn't take no brains to see that there was
something going on between them two.
When all the whispering was over, Ann and
Jamie were climbing down in that cellar
Turk had told us about earlier. Reckon
Carlos figured he had the whole thing
settled. I knew different. Nine days on a trail
through hell with that girl taught me a thing
or two. During that much time a body gets
to know another mighty good.

There was something on that girl's mind.
She'd got to figuring she was responsible for
all the trouble, and not wanting to let us get
ourselves killed on her account. Well, I
wasn't a man who figured on getting himself
killed, no matter what the reason. Trouble
was, a body couldn't convince her of that.
Eastern folk, they had a way of figuring the
law should handle things. But like Turk said,
there wasn't much of it in these parts. Ann
could handle a gun, and that worried me
some. She was a headstrong girl, and no
matter what she promised Carlos, she could
easily take it into her head to do what she
figured was her share. In fact, I was sure she
was pondering on it already. Thing of it was,
it gave me something more to worry on. I
didn't rightly know what was gonna happen
once Carlos and me took hold of this thing
by the handle, but whatever it was, it would
happen mighty fast once it got started. I

didn't want to think about Ann maybe turning up in the middle of something at the wrong time. Carlos sure enough didn't either, and it looked to me like he had even more reason than me, considering the way them two'd been getting on. It looked real serious to me, weddin' ring serious.

Well, a man didn't get no place without taking the first step, so I slipped up close to that door, my rifle at the ready. Carlos come up behind me and waited in silence while I checked through the knothole to be sure the ones we were after hadn't moved none. They proved to be very obliging gents, the two still at the table and the other one still at the bar, so I just opened the door and stepped on into the saloon real casual like. Carlos was right beside me, his rifle pointing in the direction of the man still lounging up against the bar. Mine was centered somewhere between the pair at the corner table. The place got quiet mighty quick, and when Turk brought out that shotgun from under the bar, I don't reckon there was a man in there who didn't know who we were.

'Just stand easy,' I advised in a voice just loud enough to make myself heard.

'Don't try it,' I heard Turk warning the lone gunman at the bar. 'You don't have to aim this thing,' he said holding his loaded shotgun ready, 'just point, and it's pointing at your belly right now.'

The lean, wolfish looking man at the bar brought his large hands up empty and let them rest on the bartop. 'I ain't looking to be picked up with a rake, mister,' he said quietly, 'there'll be another time.' He glanced over at me, sort of taking my measure. 'Where'd you hide the girl and kid?' he asked abruptly, not really expecting an answer. 'Around here somewheres, the way I figure it,' he smirked. I kept my mouth shut while Carlos moved between the three collecting guns and knives while Turk and me kept them quiet. It ain't in me to kill with no reason, so we herded them in the back room and left them hogtied on the floor.

That much had been easy enough, but we hadn't nowhere near taken the bull by the horns yet. I cat-footed it up to the batwings and looked out on the dark street. I motioned to Carlos, and he slipped up beside me.

The streets were empty save for a few men scattered up and down its length a good piece away, but still I kept my voice low, not wanting the whole saloon to know my figuring. 'We best go after Morton,' I told Carlos. 'No sense in cutting off a lizard's tail, it just grows back.'

Carlos touched my shoulder and gestured behind him. 'The back way, amigo?'

Me, I shook my head. 'That's what they're expecting. They'll be less likely to see us walking down the main street than slinking around out back.'

We stepped out the swinging doors together, Carlos and me, our rifles cradled casually in our arms. We drew a couple of questioning glances from further on down the street, but nothing else. The night air was cool, but as we walked I felt as if there was a piece of wet rawhide wrapped around my chest and it was starting to shrink up. My mouth felt dry as cotton. There wasn't no telling how many enemies we had in this town, and as for the law, well there just wasn't any so's anybody would notice. Me and Carlos were on our own, and it wasn't a feeling to make a man feel comfortable. There was something of a breeze stirring down between the buildings, and me and Carlos walked light-footed, our boots making only muffled sounds in the dusty street. When a man lived in the thick of the Apache most of the time he learned to step lightly, and his walk changed but a little when he hit a town.

We hadn't taken more than a dozen easy strides when I heard someone coming up fast behind us, and calling out a pair of names loud enough to wake the dead. Well, I figured those names to be the handles that pair we had tied up in the back of the saloon went by, and whoever it was at our backs was figuring us for them. Having him come up on my back thataway didn't set too well with me, but he was figuring us for his own men, so the best thing was to let him come on. With that fella bellowing like a bull in our direction, every man in town must'a been staring our way. I didn't want to pull the gun that hung from my hip or use the rifle I held out in plain view. We took a couple more strides with him shouting after us. That put us up in the shadows near a passageway between the general store and the dressmaking shop beside it. We stopped there waiting for him to come up alongside, not wanting the rest of them coyotes spread out on the street to get suspicious. Carlos stood forward some, letting his shadow fall across me while I let my hand slip unnoticed into my shirt. That little .44 derringer I was carrying felt mighty good when I wrapped my hand around it and brought it out.

That fella come up on us mighty quick after we stopped. He was short and stocky, walking with a stride that reminded me of a banty rooster. His hands swung back and forth at his sides real bossy like, and there was an angry scowl on his face that could be seen even in the dark. The broad brim of his hat shaded most of his face, but the angle of his chin stuck way out was enough to get his message across. He stopped short almost directly in front of me, his boots ringing on the wooden boardwalk. It took him more time than I expected to get himself a good look at that .44 aimed at his gizzard, and then shifted his steely gaze upwards to first my face, then Carlos's. He licked his lips and started to take a step backward.

'I wouldn't,' I said softly, my voice bringing him up short. He looked from me to Carlos and back again. 'Just keep your hands where they are,' I advised, 'and let's get off the street.' I jerked the little gun in the direction of the dark passage between the buildings.

Without further hesitation, he did as I said and the three of us disappeared into the darkness, appearing real friendly like ... I hoped. A good look at the squared off little man told me he was no gunny. Probably some cousin or another belonging to Bull Morton and figuring himself pretty handy with a gun. There was a swagger to his walk, but he wasn't of the same stripe as those we'd left in the back room of the saloon. The hitch was, a man like that could almost be more trouble than a hired gun. He was more likely to try something stupid or what he thought was heroic. A hired gun was more concerned with keeping his hide in one piece and collecting his pay.

I stayed up close beside him as we ducked into the alley, and that's where I laid the butt of the derringer alongside his head. He folded without a sound, and Carlos lowered his limp body to the dust. Pulling some piggin' strings from his pocket, Carlos tied the man's hands and feet like he was a calf ready for branding. We left him like that and slipped off behind the general store, coming out a little farther down the street so's it would look like shorty and us parted company some ways back.

It would'a worked too, if shorty hadn't come to a mite too soon and managed to squirm out on the boardwalk, making more noise than a Texas longhorn bull coming through the brush.

Well, that tore it. It wouldn't be more than a couple seconds before the whole town would know we was loose now, including Bull Morton and Ann's uncle. At least it was a comfort to think Ann and Jamie were out of their reach. That shorty, laying stretched out on the boardwalk, let out one bellow like a wounded bull and me and Carlos hit the street running like a pair of coyotes caught in the henhouse.

CHAPTER NINETEEN

Bullets snapped into the dust at our feet, but nothing came close enough to give a man call to worry. Seemed like those boys wasn't exactly sure of their targets, and didn't want to risk shooting one of their own men. Me, I didn't have that problem. I snapped off a couple of shots with the gun I'd snatched from my holster replacing the derringer. There was some satisfaction in seeing one man go down, taking the slug in his leg. Carlos and me slipped down an alleyway alongside the livery, and cut up the street heading for the second saloon and the hotel. Seemed likely that Bull Morton would be hanging out at one place or t'other. Turk'd said Bull was waiting for me to show myself. Well, I wasn't a man to do much waiting. If Morton was looking for me, he'd find me ... on my terms.

Holding up for a spell behind the gunshop, Carlos and me could still hear the angry voices behind us, and even an occasional gunshot. I couldn't figure what they were shooting at, but I was hoping they'd manage to hit a few of their own men in the confusion. Slipping my handgun back into my holster, I checked my rifle again. We stayed put for a while, hidden by the darkness, trying to figure on how to get across the broad open space that stretched out ahead of us.

Adam Tucker was over to the Lucky Horseshoe Saloon where he'd been recruiting men at fighting wages when all the ruckus Carlos and me kicked up got started. He didn't have all the money he rightly needed, but he had roughly half. So he was flashing his roll and offering half now, and half when the job was finished. The offer seemed reasonable to most, them not knowing he didn't have the other half. Six men accepted his offer right off, and a couple more were giving some thought to it. Adam'd even managed to woo away one of Morton's hired gunnies by offering more money. Where he was going to get the money he'd promised didn't bother him none. When the time came, something would turn up. It always did. He didn't figure it best to tell the men they'd be going up against Bull Morton head on, but he did let them know they were liable to run crossways of the man before their job was done. Most of them had only grunted and shrugged.

If I'd'a known then Morton and Adam Tucker had split, each with his own private army, I'd'a been a mighty nervous man.

With men of his own backing him, Adam was beginning to feel more sure of himself. The feeling pouring through him made him sit back and rear up some. Back East, he'd never had the feeling. To have men the likes of these taking orders from him gave Adam a drunk feeling of power. He was beginning to feel like nothing could stand against him. To his way of thinking, there was a whole lot to be said for the West. While it didn't exactly have the refinements of New York and Boston, it offered something that neither of them places could. Raw, savage power a man could latch onto and hold out here put a fire in Adam's blood. When he had that gold, he figured to buy himself the biggest spread west of the great Mississippi and he'd hire on enough men to populate a small town. With that kind of money, there'd be no problem to sending back East for his own entertainment.

The shooting and yelling Carlos and me started down the street got Adam's attention, and he strode purposefully to the batwings to have himself a look outside. There was a change in Adam Tucker, a change that the men he'd hired couldn't have known about, but Ann'd seen it. He wore a gun now, riding easy at his hip. In the past, he'd practiced a lot and had always been good with a rifle, but he wasn't any gunman. He could aim and shoot good enough for his purposes, and to him that was enough. The rough and wild men that he was hiring had to figure him to be one of them, or at least of the same cut, or they'd never stay on. Adam was real quick to grasp that fact, and to realize that the front that he put on would have to be a strong one.

Standing at the saloon door, his dark brown eyes scanning the blackness outside, he was trying to see where me and Carlos had gone to ground. His tall, six-foot-two-inch frame, cut an imposing shadow by the doorway, casting a cool authority on the room. I could see him standing there from the street. Behind him, the men Adam had hired kept their places, watching his back, and waiting to see what broke. The cruel, hard lines in his handsome face stood out in harsh relief in the half light at the saloon's doorway. He had changed to wearing a Western hat over thick black hair that'd grown shaggy since the last time he'd seen a barber.

'Let's go,' he said shortly to the men he'd hired, and stepped out the door. His words rang loudly in the clear night air. Carlos and me kept real quiet and watched.

Them gunnies followed along behind, tense and watchful. A crew of six hardened warriors. Men with their own separate set of rules. Men who hired out their guns to the highest bidders and let the chips fall where they may.

I saw them six and Adam Tucker coming out of the Lucky Horseshoe, and from the description Ann had given me I knew it had to be her uncle. Her uncle never wore a gun was what she told me, but I took note that there was one hanging from his hip. Sure enough looked like he had changed his mind some about guns. I was hunkered down on one knee behind the gunshop, Carlos right beside me, and my rifle cradled in my arms.

Them six with Tucker weren't no friendly Eastern businessmen. He had himself a pretty good crowd, and I figured he'd be needing more help than me if they found out he couldn't handle them. They were like a winter-starved pack of wolves, ready to turn on most anything.

With them seven moving on off down the street, things looked pretty quiet. Leastways, near as quiet as they were likely to get 'til this thing was finished. Trouble was, we'd lost the advantage of surprise that we'd had before shorty had shot off his big mouth. They knew we were somewheres about, and they were watching.

I pulled my hat a mite lower on my head to keep the light from catching my curly blond hair and marking me for Morton's guns. Hefting my rifle, I started across the dimly lit street at a trot. Well out into the open with Carlos only a few strides behind me, the shooting started.

One or two shots were snapped off quickly, and the others came like a ragged volley. Something tugged at my pants leg as I made a mad dash for cover. Out of the corner of my eye I saw Carlos catch one high up on his left leg. It gave him quite a jolt and he staggered. I pulled up in midstride to go back, saving myself from running headlong into another bullet, but Carlos was already spun around and heading back the way we come. Picking up stride, I slid in behind a horse trough, rolled down its length, and crowded up alongside the hotel's north wall. I glanced back to where Carlos had stopped, leaning against the back wall of the gunshop, and saw he was tying a neckerchief tightly around the wound. I stayed where I was a bit, able to pick out a couple of gunmen from that angle, and let loose with a few well-placed shots of my own. One of the gunnies I caught square and the rest pulled back. There wasn't much Carlos could see from his place behind the gunshop except me. I had given the situation some thought and was about to try my luck at getting back to his side when he up and lit a shuck in another direction, right into the thick of it. My breath came out in a long sigh as I shook my head. It sure wouldn't be to my liking to be the one to have to tell that boy's pa if he managed to get his brains blowed out.

With Carlos lost to me in the night shadows, I snapped off a couple more shots and turned on my heel to be moving along when I heard a window open above me and some more lead came whipping my way. Somebody was hanging out of that second floor window and keeping me pressed flat against the wall. There wasn't no time to be wasting with the rest of Morton's men knowing where I was, so I took me a chance. Rifle cocked, I took a step back and cut loose. There was a strangled cry from the window, and a man fell, like a sack of flour, to the dusty passageway at my feet. I looked down at the face as I lifted the gun from lifeless fingers and stuffed it in my waistband to be used as a spare. The pale half light cast by the hotel windows fell across the man sprawled in the dirt. Abel Jenkins. He was still wearing thick bandages from the last time we crossed trails back in the hills. Seemed to me like some folks just never learned, and it didn't look to me like he was gonna get a chance to do any more learning. I turned and slipped off alongside the hotel around to the back. I took the time to check my rifle and loaded it to the guards. It paid a man to know he was packing a full load. The gun I took from Jenkins, I loaded too and stuck it back in my belt. Coming up over those stairs, crouched low like a big cat, I tried the back door. I hadn't figured it'd be locked, and it wasn't. Easing the latch, I slipped through, closing the door behind me, making no more noise than a shadow. Walking on the outsides of my feet, Indian style, I crossed the back storeroom and moved down the narrow hallway to the entrance to the lobby. The room was empty save for the desk clerk. Stopping in the shadows, I kind of took it all in, placing the stairs, the front door, the windows and anywhere else trouble might spring from.

The wood of the stairs creaked as it took a heavy load. I glanced up, startled some by seeing the big man himself coming down them stairs. Outside, some ways off I could hear gunfire. Carlos was into something. That there was one boy who had him a lot of sand. He was smart enough too. Trouble was, there was times when he just didn't use plain sense. Experience was what he needed. He hadn't had enough of that yet, except maybe with Indians, and I was hoping he'd live long enough to get himself a lot of experience.

I stepped out of them shadows into that near empty room, and let my rifle point almost casually in Bull Morton's direction as he come off'a those stairs. There was a younger man right behind him. The younger man had himself a good-sized mustache, flinty gray eyes, and a vicious looking scar that ran across his right cheek. There was something about him that looked some like the big man in front of him, and I took him to be Morton's other son. There wasn't a flicker of emotion from either of the men on the stairway, and the desk clerk just stood quiet, his mouth hanging open.

'Just stand easy, and drop your gunbelts,' I said real quiet like.

Bull Morton stood there at the bottom of the stairs staring at me through burning green eyes for long seconds. The gray flecks stood out in his black eyebrows as he frowned and clenched his hands into ham-sized fists. Then, all of a sudden he smiled through that thick black beard of his, a few seconds later he was laughing. I watched that broad, tanned face with the flattened nose, and right ear crumpled like a piece of dried leather as it contorted into laughter. His large frame shook, but the young man behind him remained impassive as when I'd first seen him.

'You're a dead man,' Bull sneered coldly as his laughter faded. 'Why don't you lay down on the floor there and save us all a lot of trouble?'

Amiably I grinned back at him as I cocked the rifle. 'If I am,' I said pointedly, 'then so are you. I don't aim to go alone.'

The smile was completely gone from Bull's face as he loosened his gunbelt, easing it to the floor along with his son's.

'In fact,' I went on, as the gunbelts hit the wooden floor, 'you have more trouble than you know about.' Just guessing, I rambled on trying to get the big man off stride while I figured what to do with him. 'Seems like Adam Tucker didn't take kindly to your getting rid of him,' I told him, figuring there had to have been a break between the two if Tucker was out hiring on his own men. 'He's been over at the Lucky Horseshoe hiring guns. Looks to me like he's out for your scalp.'

'The hell you say!' Bull growled as he took an aggressive step forward.

I eased back a mite as the door was thrown open and a slender young woman flew into the room amid a swirl of heavy petticoats. She pulled herself up short inside the door with a squeak of surprise. I threw her a glance from where I was holding Bull and his son. She was very small with large, round eyes sunk deep in her head. Her skin was a pale white. There didn't seem to be much more of her than skin, bones, and large, china blue eyes. She didn't look to have had a healthy day in her life.

'My niece, Claire,' Bull's voice grated, 'you ain't figuring on shooting her too.'

Words started to tumble from the mouth of Claire as she went on to tell what happened. 'There was trouble down at the saloon on the far side of town, Uncle Bull.' She slowed down a mite to catch her breath, then started in again. 'That Tucker fella hit the saloon with six men. Cracked that barkeep an awful wallop on the skull, and then he found that girl you're looking for and her brother in the back room. The kid got away, but Tucker has the girl. His men killed a couple of yours along the way and another in that saloon's back room,' she said pointedly to Bull, 'but my brothers managed to slip out while all the excitement was still

218

going on.'

It didn't seem to me there was much call to keep an eye on something as small and frail as that little thing when she come in the door, even if she was Morton's niece. 'Sides, I had my hands full keeping a wary eye on a slippery snake like Morton, and there wasn't no telling what that son of his might try. But that last part that she said, about her brothers, sunk in and I threw a look in her direction. Them pretty little hands of hers were wrapped around a full-sized Colt, and that barrel was swinging around in my direction.

'Well, shoot him, Claire honey,' Bull urged quietly from the stairs.

Me, I jumped to one side as that Colt went off and flattened myself on the floor.

'No!' Cyrus shouted, jumping past his father on the stairs, missing picking up that slug by inches.

'No?' I wondered as I scuttled for cover behind the hotel desk. Seemed to me I remembered my pa telling me to never turn my back on a woman. And as far as that Cyrus went, there weren't no telling what he had on his mind. I rolled across the floor behind the desk, toppling the desk clerk. My rifle had been lost when I jumped to avoid the load that Colt was packing, and I drew my handgun as I reached the door. There hadn't been any other shots after the first, but now Bull had retrieved his gun from the stairs where it had fallen, and he snapped off a couple of quick ones as I dashed out the door into the covering darkness. Gingerly, I avoided the pools of light that poured from some of the buildings in town. There'd been plenty of shooting in town this night, but the good citizens of Tucson looked to have figured it wasn't none of their business and kept the storm shutters closed tight. There wasn't nothing for me to do but go on back to Turk's place, and get what happened out of him. Catfooting it down the main street, I slipped through the darkness like a snake through grease 'til I caught sight of somebody moving off toward the livery stables. Bull was shooting and yelling up the street a piece, sounding like a wounded grizzly, setting his dogs on me.

With gun drawn, I pulled up a little short of the livery and watched. A tall, thin man came out of the shadows dragging with him a woman I recognized immediately to be Ann. Strung out behind Adam Tucker, and in pairs were the six men I'd seen with him at the Lucky Horseshoe Saloon a short time back. They were moving mighty quick, probably not wanting to come crossways of a bunch of Morton's men. They passed beneath the lamp the livery man had left burning and went on inside. I waited a few seconds, then followed along behind them.

All around me I could hear loud voices and the sounds of running feet. In the dark it seemed most men moved quickly from place to place, always looking, but never seeing.

The door creaked as I swung it open wide enough to slip inside the livery. A lamp had already been lit and a pale yellow glow filled the inside of the room. Two of the men were already up in the loft standing watch when the door creaked at my entrance. Adam jerked Ann roughly into one of the stalls as guns exploded and I dove for the cover of a wagon, lead snapping at my heels and whipping past my head. Pulling myself up alongside the wheel, I rared up and snapped off a shot into the loft. There was a startled grunt from above, and a gun went spinning over the edge into a pile of hay on the floor. The man's partner popped up out of nowhere and drew down on me. His first slug took me high in the left thigh, sending a knifing pain through it, throwing me over backward, leaving me wide open for his next shot. Trouble was, he got overanxious and his second and third shots missed me clean. Rolling over on my belly, I took careful aim for shooting uphill, and squeezed off my shot. The hired gunman threw his arms wide and fell back out of sight. There were only a couple of horses in stalls, but they were kicking up an awful fuss with all the shooting going on around them. They were snorting and stamping so much it was hard for me to hear much else. Without wasting no time I stuffed my neckerchief inside my pants leg where the bullet had gone clean through, wincing when I touched the wound, then I slipped a couple shells into the empty chambers of my gun.

There were four others and Adam Tucker spread around the inside of that livery. I could hear an occasional footstep or the rasping sound of leather brushing against wood when one of 'em got up too close to the wall. Slipping alongside the buckboard, limping badly I worked my way over to the first stall and ducked inside it. The horses were quieting some, and I could hear a couple of Tucker's men working their way up on me, trying to put me in a crossfire. The idea didn't set too well with me. Leaning out of the stall, I snapped off a blind shot to sort of give them something to worry about. There wasn't time for a body to draw a breath before one of them answered my shot. Whoever it was threw that lead was using straw for brains, 'cause that bullet didn't come nowhere near me but it sure enough took another one of Tucker's men square.

I came to my feet with a lunge, crossing the pool of light that lamp threw with long strides, dropping into a pile of hay behind a slatted wall in the shadows. A couple of shots followed me to the ground, and I returned the fire, throwing my shots where I'd seen muzzle fire. A man fell on the fringes of the light, his gun flung far from him. He was still breathing, but he wouldn't be throwing lead for a spell. There was a flash of movement behind a stack of saddles and harnesses. I pulled the trigger and the hammer clicked on an empty chamber. Easing back into the shadows, I slipped my gun back into its holster and pulled the spare from my belt.

Long seconds passed. Only the horses' nervous stamping and the heavy breathing of the wounded man broke the silence. There were still two of them left, and Tucker. By now the whole town would know there was something going on in the livery, and it was a sure thing Bull Morton would be showing up any time.

'Hey, Matt Logan, I know it's you out there,' Adam Tucker's voice broke the silence. 'You back off, or I'll kill Ann right here.'

I leaned up against the wall. I'd been waiting for that. There wasn't no doubt in my mind that he meant it. But I wasn't fool enough to believe he'd ever let her go alive either.

'Go ahead,' I bluffed, 'if you never want to find the gold ... she's the only one knows where it's at.' I lied.

Adam Tucker didn't answer, but I could

hear one of his men moving around nearby. At the far end of the barn I heard the door creak as it was opened and closed. Either one of Tucker's men decided to head for greener pastures, or he was trying to circle around and come up on me from another direction. I worked my way forward through the hay, the stuff rasping and rattling with my every move. A gun cracked and a bullet smacked into the wooden post beside me, sending a shower of splinters down my arm. I pulled myself into a crouched position close up against the shadowed wall. Then I waited.

It couldn't have been more than a minute or two before I spotted the pair of legs showing behind the wheels of the buckboard where I'd been before. I was leading him, letting him come a little farther forward when the small side door opened and closed to my right. It was more like a feeling, I didn't really see the door open. The shadows deepened and changed for a second, and a breath of cooler air circled through the open doorway. The muscles in my legs were tightening, getting ready to move, the wound worrying at me some. I could see the horses in the livery from where I was crouched. Suddenly the sorrel tossed his head and pricked his ears. There was something coming up behind him that he didn't like. It crossed my mind that I wouldn't like it either. Slipping around the edge of the stall, I started moving into the next.

When I come around the end of that box stall, I saw that fella the same time he saw me. The silence that had been long punctuated only by footsteps and scraping exploded in gunfire as our guns did the talking. He had me cold, but he was in too much of a hurry. His shots went wild as I dove headlong onto the floor and snapped a shot up at him. It took him solid, throwing him backward into the wall. There wasn't time to see if my shot finished him as the one I'd spotted behind the buckboard came up on me from behind. Rolling, I come up on my belly, my elbows braced on the floor. It took him only a second to realize he was staring right down my gunbarrel. Anybody with a lick of sense would have quit while he was ahead, but not this gunny. That gun of his wasn't nowhere near having me in its sights, but he tried to bring it around to get off a shot. I had plenty of time. Taking a good aim I put one in his right forearm, snapping the bone. He dropped to his knees holding his injured arm and letting his gun drop to the floor with a hollow thud. I jumped up and got his gun before he could take it into his empty skull to try a pot shot at me with his left hand.

I was standing there like that, right out in the open, holding that gunny's handgun in my left hand, and my own nearly empty one

225

in my right when Tucker showed himself down near the back of the stable. He was holding Ann by one small wrist and staring in my direction. When he caught sight of me still standing and his hired guns spread all over the floor, he did the only thing a man in his position was likely to do. Swinging Ann around in front of himself, he threw down on me. I felt like a damned fool tenderfoot, my gun pointing dead center at Tucker, but I couldn't fire for fear of hitting Ann. Adam Tucker didn't have the same problem. He squeezed off a shot that slammed into my right side, staggering me, and throwing off my aim.

Ann stared at me in horror, and it wasn't hard to figure why, knowing what I looked like. Blood was already soaking most of my clothes, and now there was a bright, fresh stain, spreading out from just above my right hip. There wasn't any real pain yet, save for that leg wound I'd picked up earlier. The rest would come later, if there was a later. Ann lunged from her uncle, trying to cross the room to me. It was a fool thing for her to try, but Tucker must have figured me for a dead man 'cause he let her go, laughing, and taking a couple steps in my direction himself.

Down on my knees on the straw-covered floor, and feeling mighty weak, I braced myself against a post, and brought my gun up, firing in almost the same motion. At the last second Tucker saw it coming. The laughter died in his throat as he tried to bring his gun up fast enough for another shot when a split second realization spread across his face. I squeezed off that shot with the practice and reflex of long years behind it. My shot finished him where he stood. His only expression was a last long look of surprise.

I relaxed against the post where I'd been bracing myself as Ann rushed to my side. There was a lot of noise from the back of the livery and I took note of the man who's arm I broke only a short time ago, slipping out through the front. My mind was beginning to feel a mite foggy, but something was urging me to stay upright, while Ann was begging me to lay down and take it easy while she went for the doc.

The door at the back of the livery flew open, and through rapidly blurring vision I saw the bulk of Bull Morton appear, framed in the yellow light of the lamp. His son came in right behind him and stared at the carnage around him, then back at me. Finally, his hard, gray eyes came to rest on Ann where she kneeled in the straw beside me. Bull was holding a gun, a Colt probably, but it was dwarfed by the size of his hand, looking a lot like a toy. I sighed deeply. So after all this, it was going to end here. Bull was grinning, but he didn't make the mistake of taking his eyes off me. I wasn't dead yet, and he too had learned the hard lesson that a half dead man could sometimes be more dangerous than a healthy one. Bull chuckled kind of low and deep a couple of times, but he made sure he had his gun on us. His remaining son, Cyrus, backed off a couple of paces and drew his own gun. Looking at him through glazed, uncertain eyes I saw that gun of his pointing not at us, but at his pa. I blinked, but the view didn't change.

'We're not going to kill a woman, Pa,' I heard him say through a daze.

Bull half turned on his son, but kept an eye on me. 'She killed your brother, there ain't no reason to let her live.'

Cyrus shook his head. 'Curley Bill was poison mean, I know what he was, and you ain't going to kill that girl.'

My fogged mind was scrambling for an explanation to all this, but at the same time, through old reflex, my hand was trying to bring my gun up again. But now, suddenly it felt like a dead weight. Struggling to bring it up, my strength was leaving faster than I cared to think about, even as I knew deep inside that Cyrus wasn't going to kill his own father.

Bull knew it too, 'cause he just up and turned from his son pointing that gun dead center at me. Cyrus cocked his six-gun, the sound of it snapping loudly in the silence, and Bull jerked his head around toward his son. He stared hard at Cyrus for a spell while I was sweating and trying to bring the barrel of my gun back in line for a shot. Ann knelt beside me, her gaze fixed on the gun Bull held. Bull turned again from his son and jerked his gun around to finish us off when I finally managed to bring my own gun back into play.

Three shots ripped through the air, echoing through the livery as one. For a few seconds I wasn't quite sure what had happened. My gun had gone off, as had Bull's, but neither of us had scored a hit. Then Bull Morton fell to the floor like a toppled tree. I blinked a couple of times. It didn't make any sense. I was sure I'd missed him, and Cyrus hadn't fired.

Then Carlos came around from the side of the livery near the door, a tiny wisp of smoke still hanging from the muzzle of his rifle. He stepped quickly to Bull's side, checking to be sure the big man wasn't a threat to his back, then walked quickly over to Ann and me. Cyrus eased the hammer on his gun back in place and slipped it back in his holster as he stood staring down at his father. There didn't seem to be nothing he wanted to do. No killing, no revenge, he'd had enough of that. Most likely, he felt as if he was free for the first time.

Carlos squatted beside me and scratched

his head. 'The doctor is on his way,' he told Ann sort of quiet like. 'I sent Jamie after him.' A serious expression on his face, Carlos looked at me. 'It was not wise to come in here alone, amigo, and that last shot,' he gestured toward where Bull lay, 'you missed him clean.' Looking around the room, Carlos shook his head in wonder, then grinned at me. 'Folks say every man is entitled to one stupid mistake, it looks like you just made yours.'

I gave him a sideways grin, 'I've made a helluva lot more than one, amigo,' I told him, then just sort of eased back in the straw and let the darkness wash over me.

CHAPTER TWENTY

I didn't really get my senses back for a couple of days, but when I did, I found myself laying in a soft bed with everybody and a stranger clustered off in one corner of the room.

Heaving myself up on one elbow, and regretting it at almost the same instant, I glanced off across the room. Turk's head was all wrapped up in bandages, and Carlos had his arm in a sling, but it looked to me like I was the only one to land flat on my back.

'What the hell's goin' on?' I whispered

hoarsely.

Turk wheeled at the sound of my voice, and sprinted for my bed. 'Thought you weren't never coming back, boy!' he said cheerfully, 'but I figured it would take more than three or four slugs to keep you down long.'

I glared up at him. 'No more favors, Turk,' I said abruptly. 'We're square.'

Turk nodded vigorously as Carlos and Ann came up to the bed, but I knew better than to believe him. I also knew the next time he opened his mouth I'd be there.

'Doc,' I called past Ann and Carlos, 'he's paying the bill,' I said pointing to Turk.

Carlos looked a mite eager to tell me something. 'Amigo, we wanted you to know, because you are our best friend, that Ann and I are to be married. As soon as you can stand on your own two feet, you are to be best man.'

'Congratulations,' I shook Carlos's hand. I'd figured that to be coming. Then it hit me. 'You're going to take her back down through that hell hole we just come up through a few days back?' I asked wearily.

He nodded and shrugged. 'She liked it,' Carlos said. 'And my father, he loves her as a daughter.' His way of talking showed how proud he was. 'And, of course, Jamie will also come with us.'

Thinking of the Apache and the desert, I

just sort of let my eyes pass from one to the other and sighed.

Carlos took Ann by the hand and started to lead her from the room. 'You must rest now, but don't worry about us. We'll name the first son after you.'

Giving Turk a sharp glance, I laid back on the bed. Matthew Otero. I turned it over in my mind a bit. It had a good strong sound to it.

P(eggy) A(nne) Bechko was born in South Haven, Michigan. By her own admission she was never capable of short lengths and so it was inevitable that her first published work would be a novel. She had always loved the American West and had visited it frequently. She wrote her first Western, THE NIGHT OF THE FLAMING GUNS, at the age of twenty-two. She signed the manuscript P. A. Bechko, so it came as a surprise when her agent, who had never before spoken to her, telephoned to say that Doubleday had made an offer on it. Her editor at Doubleday was no less surprised when he saw her full legal name. However, he went on to buy four more Western novels from her.

In 1981 Bechko finally moved to where she wanted most to be, Santa Fe, New Mexico. Together with her mother and with occasional help from her brother, she went about completing from the ground up much of the home in which she lives. In addition to two original paperback Westerns for Pinnacle Books, Bechko also branched out in the 1980s to write romance novels for Harlequin, but with an authentic Western setting, such as her recent historical romance, CLOUD DANCER (1991). Her books, beginning with her Westerns, have been translated into the principal European languages, including French, German, Italian, Spanish, and Dutch. Western fiction by P. A. Bechko is now being made available for the first time in Eastern Europe. She is currently at work on a new Western story. C. L. Sonnichsen writing in EL PASO TIMES described Bechko as 'one of the few women in the business but she outdoes many of her male counterparts in fertility of imagination.'